flip the script

flip the script

the Un-Romantic Comedy

by

E.G. Thompson

WGA Registration Number : 1501681
Cover design by E.G. Thompson for
Graphics by Doc.
Photography by Carlos O'Banion
O'Banion Photography.

ISBN-10: 0615721737
ISBN-13: 978-0-615-72173-6

Dedicated to...

Anyone who said anything harsh towards the opposite sex in my presence. I thank you all!

-E.G. Thompson

Let's laugh together...

1ˢᵗ Chapter ♣

Here was cold silence, excluding the ticking of the wall clock hanging above them. Three individuals were seated in the office of Minister Orr, who sat on the executive side of his office desk. He is the pastor of a neighborhood church.

On the other side of the desk were his "patients", an attractive, recently-separated couple who were nearing their divorce. The wife is Dyanne Long, a 34-year old daycare manager and mother of two children by her husband, Ron Long, a 33-year old office manager of a big name insurance company.

The two were together since they were college freshmen attending the same school. This day, they avoided speaking to each other.

∿

Minister Orr said, "Well... there is definitely a serious lack of communication here." He faced Dyanne. "Okay, I'll start with the Misses, since no one is willing to volunteer. It looks like you have a lot to say, Dyanne."

"I just want this to end, Pastor," Dyanne said. "I'm giving up on trying to make this thing work by myself. Mr. Long is not cooperative and I am sick and tired of being the only grown-up in the family. I married a heathen."

"Please give me an example of your husband not cooperating with you."

"When I call and ask him to have a talk about our issues, he complains about the times that I choose to ask him. No time is ever good for him!" Dyanne impersonated Ron. "'Can't you wait 'til the game is over? Can I finish this sandwich, first? It's too late to talk, I got work in the morning!'" She gasped heavily after impersonating Ron. "He avoids conversation, he never wants to talk, and he makes excuses every time I ask him to talk. This is the same as when we were living together." She held up her index finger. "But, he always had plenty of time for intercourse! That's the only thing he wanted to do as a couple. Pastor, I swear, if I-"

Min. Orr interrupted. "Thanks, Dyanne. I understand. You made your point, dear." He turned to Ron. "Ronald, please respond to your wife's complaint. And tell your side of the story."

"Well, Pastor," Ron said, "I'm already annoyed by this here meeting."

"Why is that?" asked Minister Orr. "Please explain."

"Okay, see how you were able to stop her little rant? I can't do that! I can't get a word in like you just did."

"Then, now is a chance to speak. Release yourself."

"But, that's just one thing. I agreed to this counseling, because it made logical sense. Pastor Orr, you married us."

"Yes, I performed the wedding ceremony."

↝

"Okay. You spoke the words, 'You may now kiss the bride.'"

"Yes, that was me."

"Understood. So, it would seem sensible enough for you to help us with our marital problems when we need help. I get it, that's what you do. But, I'm frustrated because I can't truly express myself without being offensive." Dyanne sighed as Ron continued. "We're in a church," he said, "I can't keep it real here. Can't cuss. I can't say 'shit'!" Min. Orr remained patient, while Dyanne showed her disgust. "And she just said 'intercourse'. Who says that? She doesn't talk like that on the phone!" He adjusted in his seat. "Let's be real! She curses all the time and so do I. "And yes... I love **sex**. She's stingy with that, too, so who's not being cooperative?"

Dyanne said to Minister Orr, "You see he didn't give much of an explanation. Didn't even have enough sense to defend himself. Just complaining that he can't curse like he wants to."

Minister Orr asked, "When was the last time you two talked? Dyanne?"

"It was on our youngest child's eighth birthday," she answered. "February twelfth of this year. If you want to call it talking."

"That was about... two months ago! You two barely speak to each other at all! My goodness, we're going to have to work on that, okay?"

"I am tired of trying to talk to him. He refuses to grow up. It's like talking to a whiny child."

Minister Orr asked Ron, "Will you please tell your wife how you feel about her and your marriage?

"You have my permission to express yourself as you wish."

"Wait..." Ron said. "Are you sure about that?"

"Go right ahead."

"Alright, here goes..." He cleared his throat while turning towards Dyanne. "You make my balls hurt. You betrayed me by changing for the worse!

"You don't want to have fun anymore. You don't pretty yourself up like you used to. Just because I've seen you on the toilet, smelled your gas, and heard you snoring, that don't mean you should give up on being sexy for your man sometimes!

"As for talking, you don't want to talk. Please! You just want to yell without my interruption. Yeah, you're a sweetheart here in the church -all prissy in front of the preacher- but that's just a front!

"And how are you going to fault me for wanting sex? You were my wife!

"I don't have a battery-operated buddy in a bag like you do!

"And when you finally do agree to sex, I swear it gets dryer every time! It gets dryer every time the wind blows! I bet I could strike a match in it! The thrill is gone and so am I!"

Minister Orr did not anticipate this type of response. "Ron... wow," he said. "It looks to me that you are not interested in finding a solution that both of you can work with.

At least not for now.

"But at the same time, sex seems to be your main complaint. I'm not sure if that is reasonable grounds for divorce." He turned to Dyanne. "Maybe we can get a more in-depth analysis by hearing what you have to say to your husband. You may also express yourself as you wish. Lord help me."

"I have nothing to say to Ronald," Dyanne said.

"Dyanne, I know you're upset. Just let out all that you are holding inside. I won't look at you any different. I'm not here to pass judgment."

"Well... If the kitty is dry, then someone needs to do a better job with the tongue. I'm not saying any names, but it would help if someone did not treat the kitty cat like corned beef on rye. You know?" Diane spoke these words without facing Ron. "But if that is too complicated, then that same someone should at least find some special way to keep their cucumber ripe. Not wilted like a string bean, but completely ripe."

Ron yelled out, "Don't even try it! You know damn well I stay hard!" He looked up to the heavens. "Excuse me, Lord..." Again, he faced Dyanne and pointed her out. "But, that's a lie!"

"I wouldn't say 'hard'," Dyanne said, still looking away from Ron. "Hardly hard. Maybe kind of stiff, but not hard. Must be where our son gets his bad posture."

"Hey! Well, how can you expect 'someone' to not be slumped over after crossing the desert? As a matter of fact, your head game ain't all that, either!"

Dyanne finally turned facing Ron. "Why you lazy dick mutha-"

"Okay, okay!" Minister Orr intervened. "That's enough. I thought I could handle the language, but I was badly mistaken." He was clearly disappointed. "I am surprised. Not judging, but... surprised. I have always seen you as a wise couple. Accomplished. And educated." He was baffled. "But, you are showing me a different side of yourselves. This petty talk about sex, I don't understand it completely. There seems to be something missing."

Dyanne asked Min. Orr, "If your heart is detached from your spouse, can you say that you are truly with that person? When you can no longer keep your vows? When you are willing to leave that person for the smallest of reasons? When you can't wait for death to do you part?" She placed her hand on her chest. "This is how I feel. I want more out of life than this. I have grown, but apart from him. He was perfect for young Dyanne back in the day, but not good enough for the woman I have become. I've outgrown him."

"Oh really!" Ron shouted. "Alright, here's the deal, Pastor. When you performed our wedding, she was two months pregnant. I married her, because she wanted to be married. It all started with her best friend, Wanda."

Wanda Anderson-Lewis was Dyanne's best friend since Junior High School. A knock-out beauty in her past days. She had been married three times by the age of thirty. She had been engaged five times. She is divorced once again.

Ron described what precipitated his marriage to Dyanne with a long story.

"Wanda had this big wedding with the horse carriage and all kinds of fancy stuff," Ron said. "The most expensive wedding I have ever seen! And the shortest marriage, too.

"Young Dyanne, here, was the Maid of Honor. All the bridesmaids were debating on who was next to get married. This built the anticipation of... the bouquet toss!

"Now, young Dyanne had never been a superstitious person in all the years I've known her. But on this day, she was determined to catch that bouquet to become... the next bride!"

As Ron told this story, he went into narration like a Great Moments in Sports television program. One would think a marching band was playing in the background.

"All the bridesmaids were lined up, then all of a sudden, a big husky woman who stood about six feet two and three-hundred-something pounds made her way into the lineup saying, 'That bouquet is mine! Move outta my way!'

"But young Dyanne was focused. She saw all the glamor, the attention, and wanted it for herself. As most women do. Nothing was going to stop her!

"Wanda stands in front. Turns her back towards the eager women. She swings her arm up with flowers in hand. The women start to scream! They look into the air, but saw only the sky. It was a fake throw!

"The desperate women were angry at the bride for fooling them like that. Everyone else thought it was funny, but not them.

"Wanda, the bride, gets set again. The women anxiously await. Not one blink between them.

"But, young Dyanne was a High School Volleyball State Champion! And she was poised! She kicks off her high heel shoes,

↝

positioning herself like she used to when preparing to spike the ball over the net.

"The bouquet is in the air! Young Dyanne leaps high into the air like Jordan! Tongue hanging out like His Airness! Posterizing the big woman! She has the bouquet!

"But when she brings it down, the large hand of the husky woman reaches and grabs it! Young Dyanne holds on saying, 'I had it first!', but that meant nothing to the large lady at hand.

"The two fell to the ground with the bouquet. Pedals everywhere! But it wasn't about the condition of the bouquet, it was the condition of standing alone with the bouquet!

"Then, something happened. Young Dyanne suffered a wardrobe malfunction! The aggressiveness of the battle was too much for young Dyanne's attire. How could she secure her prize capture while avoiding exposure of her goods?

"Young Dyanne was caught in a dilemma. She had to react quickly! The groomsmen looked on waiting for something to pop out!

"Young Dyanne rolls over and pulls the big woman closer to her with one arm! Who knew she had so much strength? She has the eye of the tiger!

"She opens her mouth and bites the wrist of the plus-sized phenom! She locks on like a pit bull until her opponent releases her grasp of the bouquet!

"She stands to her feet in victory holding up the bouquet in one hand and holding her shoulder strap with the other hand! In her eyes, she was destined for marriage!"

Ron finished his story with a less enthusiastic tone. "Then soon after," he said grumbly, "it was the single men's turn. We stood there, reluctantly, while the groom removed the garter from his bride's thigh.

"The groom turns around, tosses the garter over his shoulder. It's in the air. Whatever.

"We looked up. Our hands at our sides. And we watched that garter go from out of the air, all the way down until it hit the

↝

ground. Thud!

"We looked at each other wondering who would have the nerve to pick up that garter. Then a voice from beyond said, 'Ron! Pick up the damn garter!' Guess who that was...

"Afterwards, she started using words like 'forever' and 'always'. And now, thirteen years later, here she is talking about outgrowing someone."

Minister Orr shook his head. "I cannot believe... that I just sat here and listened to all of that." He gathered his things. "Look, I've heard enough for today.

"I might just cancel all of my other meetings so I can clear my thoughts."

"Wait, please," Ron plead.

"What is it, Ronald?"

"I've had... relations not too long ago. With another woman. I thought that since we were separated, it was not the same as if we were still living together in the same house.

"I mean, Dyanne always says that we're no longer a couple. And that we have no true marriage other than what's on paper. You see our attitudes for yourself." Dyanne turned away. "We have no desire to get back together. We're just concerned about being who we need to be as parents. We can be decent parents, but we're terrible as a married couple.

"We don't like to be bad examples of husband and wife for our children. I have the same questions as Dyanne does. Do we still call this Holy Matrimony? Aren't we divorced internally?" Dyanne ducked her head, saying nothing.

"Now I see what really has Dyanne upset," Minister Orr said. "This is very saddening to hear. I had high expectations for you two." He wiped the sweat from his forehead with a handkerchief and sighed. "Separation is temporary and you may think that it's best for you to divorce, but you should give life more time to show you things, first. Now, I'm not saying that you can't go your own separate ways, but you only know your current circumstances. This could be premature." He faced Ron. "Brother Ron, fornication is a sin. And in your case, it's still adultery. You may disagree, but... oh, never mind." Min. Orr waved Ron off, then started to think. "I have an idea. This is something I learned years ago. I want you two to come back tomorrow evening. It'll be brief. Bring your wedding rings. Prepare to swap them."

Ron shouted, "Hey! You want me to let go of my ring? How else am I supposed to pick up women?"

2ⁿᵈ *Chapter* ⚜

*I*t was early in the morning at Ron's workplace. Ron supervises the automobile coverage team. He crept to the cubicle of Carla Stone, a single, attractive team member of his group who is in her mid twenties.

Carla spoke while looking away as she typed on her keyboard. "Good morning, Ron. I know it's you."

"Alright, Carla," Ron said after just making it to her cubicle, "tell me how you do that every morning. When I get just about one yard away from your cube, you manage to call me out every time. No matter how quietly I step."

"That's just it. You have a certain way of walking when you're up to something."

⤳

"Is that so?"

"When it's something business-related, you walk up to me at a normal pace. But when you're trying to be smooth, you start off normal to fool everyone else, then you shorten your stride the closer you get to my cubicle. Ron, you do it just about every morning."

"Okay, you got me. I just wanted to see how you wore your hair today, that's all." He pinched a lock of her hair. "When you pin it up, it's nice. But, you look even better with your hair laying down. Something about it sets the mood around here."

"No, if anything, it puts you in the mood to flirt. But that's you. I'm not knocking it, I'm used to it. So anyway, how is your wife?"

"Same way she was the last time you asked me. She is content. And single. Just not legally, yet."

"Meaning that you're still married."

"Look. Last names, joint filings, and government paperwork don't make the marriage official or not. We do. Divorce, according to man's law, is all about money. That's it. You split up, you pay us." He pointed out a news article about a famous couple who were splitting up and had no prenuptial agreement. "See that?" Ron continued. "We need less government! And I thought that marriage was a religious institution. Well then, we need to separate church from government!"

"Oh my Gosh! I see what's your problem, Ron. You don't seem to take things seriously enough. Either that, or you hide your feelings behind your bizarre sense of humor. Besides, have you talked to Nadine today?"

"Nadine? Why are you asking me about her?"

"Come on now, Ron. Women talk. You've been hitting on all the ladies in here since you first got separated." She giggled. "We were laughing about it in the lunchroom, but Nadine got quiet. Then she left. We all see it. Something happened between you

↷

two, didn't it?"

"Oh please! She just doesn't want to gossip like the rest of you."

"Nadine? Okay, then how come in one minute you are working closely together, and then the next minute, you're barely speaking? I see embarrassment. And guilt."

"You assume. That's all. Assuming just makes an ass of you and me. Ass-u-me! And how can you say I hit on all the women here? I sure as hell didn't hit on Lu-"

Interrupting was the distant voice of Luann Westoff, singing out, "Mister Long!"

Luann is Ron's geeky, badly-dressed assistant. She has always been attracted to Ron, but respected his marriage. When she heard about his possible divorce, she behaved even nicer towards him. She was excited to see him, as usual.

"Hi Luann," Ron said with a half grin.

Luann wore a big smile. "How is your day, so far?"

Ron looked at his watch. "It's been a promising two hours, Luann. I was just

↖

telling Carla here." He was anxious to leave the area. "So, I'll be heading back to my office. I'll be there for a... while. You ladies have a good day!"

Luann cheerfully waved "bye" to Ron, then turned and winked at Carla, signaling how good-looking she thinks Ron is. Carla patronized her with a less enthusiastic grin of her own. Luann didn't notice Carla's disposition and remained excited.

♀

Dyanne started her work day at Morning Glories Daycare. In her company were two of her employees, Yolanda and Mandy. Parents were dropping off their children.

Dyanne greeted the parents, then paused. One particular couple caught most of her attention. They were a newly-wed couple who brought their two kids together. She could see the love between the four of them. This reminded Dyanne of what she had with Ronald in their earlier years. Her smile slowly morphed to a gloomy frown. Yolanda noticed.

↝

"Dy, are you okay?" Yolanda asked.

"Oh, I'm fine," Dyanne replied.

"No you're not. Look, Dyanne, now is the perfect opportunity to give yourself some time off. You need it!"

"But the kids-"

"Mandy and I can run this on our own while it's so close to Spring Break. It's been slow and Mandy is out of school for now."

"I can't keep my mind off of things at home. That won't help."

"Then, leave the house! Go to the beach or something! Put on something cute! After two kids, you still look good, girl!" She put her hands on her hips. "Look at me, I'll turn forty-three in two months. You think I'm gonna just let these hot young studs pass me by? Hell no!" Mandy listened while Yolanda persuaded Dyanne. "When I decided to live my life, I forgot all about the ex. That bum. But, you might want to do something about that hair, first." She raked her fingers across Dyanne's coarse hair. "It's a mess. Seriously. A man would get arthritis trying to run his fingers through that."

"I agree with Yolanda," Mandy said. "We got this. You should extend your weekend. Have fun!"

Dyanne responded, "Yeah, I was thinking about letting the kids stay at their grandparents' this weekend. Maybe, they'll take them earlier."

"Now you're talking!" Yolanda said. "Don't worry about us, hon. We know that you're going through some things, so it's okay. You're ruining the atmosphere with that moping around, anyway."

Dyanne smiled. "Then, I'll take tomorrow off. And Friday. Get rid of the kids, hit the salon. Manicure, pedicure, massage... and the beach!" The ladies cheered. "Okay, but for now, let's set up for these little ones!"

♂

Heading to Ron's private office was James Macon, supervisor of the mailroom and Ron's best friend of ten years. James was recently married and yet to have any children. Ron helped James get the job that he has. He knocked on the office window for Ron to signal him to come inside.

James greeted Ron before closing the door behind himself. "Hey Ron. Good morning!"

"What's up, buddy?"

"Uh, I want to bring to your attention these accusations that I am hearing around the office. It's some word about you and Nadine?"

"First of all... Jay, you can speak to me like normal, man. What's all this, 'bring to your attention these accusations?'" He laughed. "It's me, man! No one can hear us. So, what are they saying about me and Nadine?"

"That... you must have slept with her. She <u>is</u> acting different. She's not saying much, either. I'm used to her being talkative and gossipy." Ron said nothing. "She is so distant now. After you two went out that other night, what happened? Did you mess around with her? You can tell me, bro."

"Yeah," Ron said, "but it was just for that night. We didn't plan it. It just... happened."

"You're joking. For real?"

"I never thought I would ever say those words, but it's true. I told Dyanne about it. Now I know for sure that it's over."

"I can't believe this! And you let Dy know?"

"Yeah she knows. But, I don't want this word to travel throughout this whole building. It can't leave this room."

James paced back and forth. "Oh no. Damn, Ron! Okay look, I'll cover for you if this spreads too wide. I know company policies are against you two hooking up. Can't let the boss find out. But dammit, man!"

Ron was nonchalant. "Thanks, Jay."

↯

3rd Chapter

Once again, the wall clock was ticking inside Minister Orr's office, but this time, the ticking sound was interrupted with chiming at 6:00pm. Minister Orr held up both wedding rings in his hands as the Longs sat on the opposing side of the desk.

"I've seen marriages come and go," Minister Orr said to begin his speech. "Some lasted for weeks. Some for decades.

"What determines the longevity is often the purpose. Most of us marry, because we are expected to. And when we feel the emotion of love, we tend to think that is our cue to begin taking steps toward what we've been hoping for.

"Some might say it is the natural order of things. But, they don't realize the truth about what's natural. Nature tells us to procreate. Period.

"Marriage was invented to maintain order and discipline. A pledge between husband and wife. Proof in who and what they are." Ron started to doze off. His head rocked back and forth.

Minister Orr stood up. "These rings; these are symbolic of many things. But these things are determined by those who wear them. They can symbolize unity or captivity. They can stand for sacrifice or interdependence. Or all of these.

"But, if you ask every couple, you will get different answers. One word that is commonly used is Love. Well, Love is more than that. Let me tell you about Love."

Ron heard the last sentence in the midst of his dozing off, then complained. "I thought you were already talking about love! You said it'll be brief!"

"Ron, I listened to your long story, now

〰

listen to mine! It's for your own good! Just be patient like Job." He brought attention to a photo of his wife. "Forty-two years ago, I met Pearl," Minister Orr said. "She was nothing that I dreamed of. I was nothing that she dreamed of. We didn't really like each other. Why? Well, no reason other than that we didn't fit each others' criteria.

"I wanted a girl who was slim, with beautiful silky hair, and dressed like a lady. Pearl was neither of those, but she wanted a jock. The pro athletic type." Ron's eyes were getting heavy again.

Minister Orr continued, "And as you can see, I was never close to being that guy. I was short and stubby. And when I tried to fit in with the group that I desired to be in, I was rejected.

"I was far from being what I thought my dream girl would want. I tried out for the football team, but couldn't run with those guys. Pearl tried out for the cheerleader squad. That was a mess." Ron snored, then he woke back up. Dyanne was pissed.

"So, we found ourselves sitting on the sidelines during a game," Min. Orr said. "At first, we wouldn't sit closely together. We didn't want anyone to see us together.

"Then, the game got exciting! It was a close one! The team was down by just a field goal with less than a minute remaining. It was so loud, we couldn't hear the whistles or the calls that were made in the game." Ron was asleep with his head leaning back and mouth wide open. "Then, the crowd started getting pushy. She was too short to see over the people standing on the bleachers in front of her. I could barely see, myself.

"Since I had compassion for her, I went to her and asked her, 'Do you want a boost on my back so you can see the game?' And she said yes. I tell you, that was the longest less-than-a-minute I had ever experienced!"

Ron woke up again. "Amen! Amen..."

"It took a lot of strength to hold her up there like that," Min. Orr said. "But, I was not going to let her down! She has been

↝

rewarding me ever since." Dyanne was visibly moved by the story.

Minister Orr's voice began to escalated with excitement. "The moral is, we found perfection through our imperfections! We lacked vision as individuals, but she became my eyes when I became her strength!

"Love brought us together through living! We didn't plan it, we planned against it! But Love said 'No'! And when **that** Love brings two together, no power can stop them!

"Ron! You were not strong enough! You were to hold her high and protect her, even from your own potential harm! And you let her down!"

Dyanne cried out, "Preach, Pastor!"

"Dyanne!" Minister Orr replied in a preachy tone. "You need more perspective!" Dyanne froze. "Don't look surprised! See, you must understand his position as well! You have every right to have expectations, but at some point, you must acknowledge his requests! As he must acknowledge yours!" He calmed down and wiped his mouth and face with his handkerchief. "It's about teamwork. When my wife and I became one, it was not a matter of settling. It was a change in our perception on things.

"And if marriage was never invented, we would still be committed to one another." Minister Orr gave Ron's ring to Dyanne, and Dyanne's ring to Ron. "I want you two to look at those rings and think about what you said when you presented them. Put these rings under your pillows tonight."

"Like for the tooth-fairy?" Ron asked skeptically. "Come on, Pastor!"

"Peculiar actions reflect freedom of the mind," the minister said. "Do things out of the norm every now and then. And do so without thinking much about it. You already do that for sin, so why not do it for something righteous?

"Now, before you go to bed... <u>alone</u>, I want you to hold the rings and look at your reflections and say this:

"Mirror, make things clearer; I drew

farther, bring me nearer"

"Oh my god!" Ron shouted. "Are you for real? What scripture is that? Are you part of some secret cult? You a Mason?"

Minister Orr replied in an aggressive tone. "Your disbelief shows your inability to see beyond your own understanding! I already told you about peculiar actions!

"It's not about the rings, the bed, the tooth-fairy, or any of that! When you do it, believe me, your mind will wonder at night. Trying to make sense out of what you just did. But, your subconscious thinking will take over in your sleep without your conscious interruption. Ron, just try it!"

Ron was feeling doubtful. "Okay, okay. Hopefully, I'll sleep well with my wonderful dreams. I'll do everything just as you said." He said sarcastically. "I'll tell you how it went."

Elsewhere, Luann Westoff exited the city transit bus after a late day of work. The bus stop is just across the street from the house where she resides. This house looks tacky on the outside with unusually bright colors, resembling Luann's taste of style, which coincided with how she wears her clothing. She was holding a package in a large paper bag.

The front porch has a wheelchair ramp connected. She walked to the porch and picked up the sales papers that were left there since earlier that morning. There is a bird feeder hanging above. She inspected the empty bird feeder, then proceeded to the door.

Airing on an old television in the front room was a classic black & white movie. Luann's mom sat there watching the romantic story. She is a disabled senior citizen who constantly sits in front of the TV watching classic films. She also suffers from dementia. She's in her late stages of the illness.

Out of four children, Luann was the only one who took care of her mother. She is the youngest of her siblings and the only one who has not married. Luann walked inside.

Luann greeted her mother. "Hi mom!" Luann's mom grunted. "I brought you your favorite cheesecake!"

Luann's mom shouted, "Cheese gives me gas!"

"Mom, you don't remember telling me you wanted cheesecake earlier?"

"Naw I didn't say I want cheesecake! I said red velvet! You don't remember! Always forgetting!"

"So, what do you want me to do with this? I can't waste it."

"Give it to Sparky!"

"Mother, Sparky is a dog. That is not something you feed a dog."

"He'll eat it!"

"No! Besides, mom, Sparky ran away weeks ago. I told you this already."

"Ran away? He wouldn't run away like that! He's a smart dog! You're lying!" As Luann's mom said this, she hit Luann with her stick, using the little strength she had.

"Ow! Mom! I am a grown woman! Stop

hitting me with that thing!"

"I won't! You go find Sparky and feed him that cheese! I don't want it. I want red velvet! Always forgetting! I bet you'll remember this ass whooping!" She hit her again.

"No! I need to fill the bird feeder, mom. That's what I am going to do. And Sparky is not here anymore!"

"Stop bringing sweets and bring home a sweetie! Look at you. Where did I go wrong with you?" She pointed at Luann. "You're the only child of mine who stays lonely. Isn't that a shame! All of them married, not you. You got your daddy's nose, that's why."

"You know what? You need your medication, Mother. You are saying some really mean, hurtful things."

♀

Later at the Longs' residence, Dyanne and her two kids, Ronald III and Marla, sat at the dining room table eating their meals.

Dyanne asked the children, "So, are you kiddies ready for the weekend with your

~↗

grandparents?"

"Yes!" said Marla.

Ronald III was less enthusiastic. "Not really. You know how Granddad is. It's like I'm in the military when he's around. He spoils Marla."

"Come on now, Ronnie," Dyanne said. "Colonel Long can't help it. He's just stuck in his days of being in the Marines. He wants you to be strong. A leader."

"I just wish he would let up, sometimes. He goes to bed early, then wakes up early. He wears combat boots with his pants tucked in them. Who does that?"

"Everyone is not like you, Ronnie. And you better not prank Granddad like you did last time! No firecrackers! It's not funny having that man duck for cover like that." Ronald III snickered. "You know he fought that war. And I know where you get these ideas from!"

"Speaking of... it looks like you cooked too much food again, Ma. There's only three of us here. Leftovers, leftovers."

Later that night, Dyanne clicked on the bathroom light. She was dressed in her night clothes. She looked into the mirror, holding the ring she once placed on Ron's finger.

She took a deep breath and said, "Mirror, makes things clearer. I drew farther, bring me nearer."

Dyanne lifted her pillow in the bedroom and placed the ring underneath as the minister instructed. She laid down and looked at the empty space on the other side of the bed. Then, she grabbed the pillow from that side and hugged it as she fell asleep.

♂

Ron lounged in his apartment suite while chatting on the cellphone with his younger brother, Aaron, who has the reputation of being a playboy. This apartment building is where Ron moved after his separation with Dyanne.

"Alright, little bro," Ron said, "we'll hang out tomorrow night. Later!" Ron hung up,

↝

then called Dyanne's house, his former place of residence. The phone rang on the other end.

The answering machine came on with a greeting from Dyanne. "You have reached us, but we're not available at this time. If you are calling for the man who used to live here, you have the wrong number. Please hang up and try a different number. Not this one." The machine beeped.

Ron left his message. "Hey, uh, I heard the kids were going to my parents' place tomorrow. Um, that's good to know. Well, uh, I would like to see them, first. Especially Ronnie. I want to talk with him before my dad gets to him. Just a little man talk, that's all. Well... I hope you-"

The machine cut Ron's message short. He reached into his pocket and took out his wife's ring. There was a mirror in the apartment living room. He glanced at it, then shook his head.

Ron said to himself, "You got to be kidding me. I don't even remember what I said. That was... thirteen years ago. Oh well, here goes..." Ron was dumbfounded. He grabbed his cellphone again.

A sound clip of church music played through the small speaker of Minister Orr's cellphone. The bedside light was turned on. Minister Orr was in bed with his wife laying next to him.

He answered, "Hello?"

"Pastor!" Ron said. "Now, what was I supposed to say again? Something about clear mirrors or something like that?"

"Goodness gracious, Ron! It's late!"

"Sorry, Pastor. I should've written it down. My bad."

"The words are, 'Mirror, make things clearer. I drew farther, bring me nearer'. Write it down!"

"I got it. Thanks!"

Ron looked at his reflection again, after hanging up. He hesitated before opening his mouth, pulled out his cellphone once again, and redialed...

"Ron!" Minister Orr yelled. "I swear, come

↝

Sunday morning, I'm giving you a wake-up call! Very early!"

"Oh, I'm sorry, Pastor! But, which do I do first? The pillow thing or the mirror poem?"

"It doesn't matter! Just do what comes naturally!"

"Okay, good! I'll do that. As strange as it may-"

"Goodnight, Ron!" He hung up the phone.

Dyanne slept on one side of her King-sized bed just as she did when Ron occupied the other side. Ron slouched across the full-sized bed in his apartment bedroom.

During their lonely nights, they both had memories of their love-making. Next, their wedding. Then, some of the first dates they had together. Then, the first time they met. And lastly, everything went blank.

❥

♣ Chapter 4ᵗʰ

*J*ames Macon was waiting inside the lobby for Ron's car to pull up to the insurance agency. He checked his watch from time to time. Ron finally arrived and parked in his designated space.

As soon as Ron walked through the door, James spoke to him. "Ron! Things are getting out of hand! I'm trying to keep it low key."

"What?" Ron asked. "Why is it so difficult?"

"It's Nadine, man. You know how she likes to run her mouth all day. That's the last woman you should've messed around with! I don't know what you were thinking!"

"Really? Damn... where is she?"

"In the lunchroom, where they do their little female bonding."

↝

Moments after, Ron and James peeked around the edge of the doorway to spy on the women. The atmosphere was a bit rowdy with Nadine leading the hype. She was surrounded by three of her female coworkers. Her antics were keeping the women riled up.

Nadine constantly bragged. "Yeah girl, I had him sweatin'! **Told** you I knew how to put it down! See, these guys are really freaks, but they play like they're so innocent. You should see him behind closed doors!"

Ron and James walked in on the ladies to surprise them. "Ladies!" Ron said. "I hope we're making progress, today. Especially in auto claims. Nadine, can I talk to you for a brief moment?" The quietened women looked concerned for Nadine as she walked away with Ron. They separated themselves from everyone.

When the two entered Ron's office, he asked Nadine, "What the hell are you doing? Are you trying to get us fired?"

"I'm sorry," Nadine replied, "I was out of line. It won't happen again. I can make it up to you later, if you'd like. Take you somewhere nice. Get your mind off of stress."

"Hold on! We promised not to do that again! Don't start switching things up on me, Nadine." He rubbed his forehead. "I knew it was a mistake to hang out with you after work," he said. "Damn! And why are you acting this way? Are you sprung?"

"Hey, I'm not sprung by any means! You got the wrong chick! And you need to stop acting so high and mighty! You are not all that! Later!"

Nadine left the office. Ron leaned back in his chair wondering how did things go so badly.

Moments later, Carla walked into his office. She was dressed more provocative than usual. Her hair wasn't pinned up this time.

"Carla!" Ron said. "Whoa, uh, you let your hair down. And the outfit..."

↬

"Is it too revealing?" Carla asked.

"No, it's just right, actually."

Carla walked to the office window and closed the blinds. "I don't understand what you see in Nadine," she said. "She's lame. Phony. Drives a station wagon. Shouldn't you have higher standards than that?"

"Oh, so now you're concerned about me. And you don't know if anything happened between me and Nadine."

"Well, what do you think about me?" Ron glanced at her cleavage. Carla noticed this and smiled.

"Don't you know already?" Ron asked. "I think you're a perfect ten!"

"Damn, baby, I thought you were shy. Do me a favor and unbutton your shirt. Let's see what you got."

"Is that it? You closed the blinds just to ask me to show what my chest looks like?" He pondered. "Wait... This is a prank, isn't it? How about you open your shirt first, smarty-pants..."

"How do I know you won't get me caught

up? Luring me in here like this."

"Are you kidding? Why would I do that?"

"Okay. If you don't tell, then I won't tell the head boss about you and Nadine."

"Huh?"

Carla began to open her blouse. Ron's eyes were wide open as he anxiously awaited. As soon as Carla's top was completely open, Ron came from behind his desk and yanked her to him. Carla looked surprised. She was amazed at how he lost control so suddenly. This intensified her loins overwhelmingly!

Ron unfastened his clothing along with Carla's, as he kissed her lips. They both flopped onto his reclining leather office chair. Carla sat on top of Ron and started grinding on him.

On the office wall clock, almost thirty seconds passed by while Carla trash talked. "Whose is it!" she shouted. "You never had it like this! Oh! I'm cumming!"

"Coming where?" Ron asked. "What? Already? But, it was only..."

↝

Carla's hair whipped Ron's face as she boasted. "Take...that!" She panted. "Who's... your... momma! Woo!" Then suddenly, she was through. She leaned on him, perspiring as if she ran a mile. Carla got up off of Ron to button her clothes back on. She wrung the sweat out of her hair like a mop that was soaking in warm water.

Carla gasped. "Wow that was good! Woo! You are my type of dude!"

"I don't understand what just happened," Ron said. "I mean, it seemed like sex, but... you're finished already? I'm good, but not that damn good!" He looked down, then back up. "Look at me, I'm still standing up down here! Can I get a nut?"

"Next time, sweetie. I can't do it right now. We got work to do, right? We can't sex all day when there are clients to take care of." Ron had a confused look on his face as his office door closed. Carla was gone.

♂

Dyanne was getting her hair done at the local beauty salon. Conversing in the salon was Barbara, who is the owner; Janie, her assistant stylist; and two of her customers. Barbara has been Dyanne's beautician for many years.

One of the customers was reading a Cosmopolitan magazine with a man on the front cover. The other customer was reading an LQ magazine. LQ stood for Ladies' Quarterly as opposed to Gentleman's Quarterly.

A song played on the radio called, "Swing it! Swing it!" This song was performed by the unattractive, out-of-shape female rapper who went by the name, "Lil' Big-Boned". Her voice was heavy and muffled while she rapped the lyrics. She would become a little short of breath between bars within the song, but that never hurt her sales. Her shtick was being a big girl who could get the men she wanted, because of her fame and the money she makes.

Barbara complained, "These songs today have no class. Listen to this... 'Swing it, swing it'. And this woman calls herself Lil'

↝

Big-Boned? What type of name is that?" She listened closely to the words of the song for a moment. "Oh my goodness! And the guys dance right along with it! Swing this, swing that. How much swinging can a woman take?"

One of the customers said, "I don't know, but I'll take as much swinging as I can get!" They laughed.

Janie said, "Well, I think all of us would. But, there's a time and a place for this type of music. They play this all day long. I agree with Barbara. It's too much!"

"Amen!" Dyanne righteously replied.

Janie said to Dyanne on the contrary, "But in your case, Dy, you should have something swinging around you by now. How long has it been?"

"Excuse me? I'm in the era of Self Love. Realizing the jewel that I am. A man must prove himself worthy to swing **anything** around me." After a long pause, the salon was filled with laughter from what Dyanne claimed.

↜

Another customer said, "Okay... Good luck with that!"

The women laughed again. Dyanne looked around wondering what was so funny.

"So Dyanne," Janie asked, "where are you headed after this? You're getting all prettied up for something, right? You're single now. Who are you trying to scoop up?"

"No one in particular. Just seeing who's out there these days. And you know, Janie, you're right. I am... single again." Dyanne smiled with confidence.

Back at the insurance company branch office, James Macon entered Ron's room unannounced while Ron was fixing his neck tie. "Ron! What's going on, bro?"

"What? What are you talking about, Jay?"

"Jeremy just said that he saw Carla leaving this office with her blouse buttoned up wrong! The guys were talking about it in the mailroom. I thought I'd check with you.

What's going on?"

"Okay, well, Carla is hot. As you know. She came in and opened her top, so I... I hit that. I think."

"You think?"

"Yeah, well, it only lasted for about half a minute. She was a bit ecstatic."

"I bet she was! Look at how easily you gave it up!" He folded his arms. "Man, since the separation, you've gotten real sleazy! Throwing your stuff around like it's free holiday sausage! And for what? Thirty seconds of pleasure?" Ron was totally dumbfounded. "I've been trying to cover for you, Ron, but I can't risk my job for you! Even though you helped me get this job, I got a wife to take care of!"

"Well, James-"

"And what would I tell her? Oh, I lied for Ron, but these young-minded women told on him anyway? Then we both got eliminated? No way!"

"I understand, James. I'm not going to get you involved in this anymore. I will handle these matters myself." Ron rubbed his chin, thinking. "I already took care of Nadine. And Carla probably just faked it anyway."

"Faked it? Faked it?" James laughed loudly. "You are too funny, Ron! I swear!" He left saying, "Faked it... ha, ha!" Again, Ron looked confused.

Chapter 5ᵗʰ

The time was 11:30am. Carla, Nadine, and two other female employees were gathered at the lunchroom table. These young women spoke in their lowered tones.

"Nadine was right!" Carla said. "Ron is a big nympho! All you have to do is pull out your boobs and you got him! He'll be right on it! He's Mr. Long alright. You should've seen how I was hittin' it!"

One of her coworkers responded, "I don't know, Carla, you were out of there pretty quick." The women laughed at Carla.

"Whatever!" Carla said. "I couldn't be in there all day. I put in work, though. He'll never forget what happened in there."

"You can have that dude," Nadine said. "I already got what I wanted from him."

The other lady employee showed her disappointment. "Wow, and I had so much respect for him. I thought he was the masculist type." She scratched her head. "Why is he like that? So promiscuous! Maybe he was molested as a child."

Nadine replied, "Hell, I don't know. All I do know is I sure was abusing that stick! Swing it, Swing it! Swing it, Swing it!" The women, excluding the one disappointed coworker, laughed along with her.

"He's just reacting to his issues with his wife," Carla said. "He's still Ronald, just vulnerable right now. So if you want it, you better get it while it's hot."

Ron was out on a stroll during his lunch break. He wore his dressed shirt without the tie, with his sleeves rolled up, and his two top buttons opened. As he walked, a man and his lady passed him by. The lady glanced at Ron over her shoulder as he passed them. Her boyfriend noticed and nudged her with his elbow for looking.

↝

Then, a car slowed down, nearly causing an accident. Ron looked to see if this was someone he knew, but it was just a lady who was observing and admiring his appearance.

Afterwards, another lady, a jogger, skipped up to him. "Oh my!" she cheered in favor of his profile. "Look at you! Where do you work out?"

"Oh thanks!" Ron said. "There's a fitness center at my job. Sorry, I would talk with you, but I'm in a hurry. It's my lunch break."

"Really? Where do you work? Which building?"

"I gotta go. Sorry!"

The jogging lady murmured under her breath as he started to leave, "Lying ass bitch."

Ron continued on his stroll. On the side of the street where he walked, there was a construction site. Construction workers, who are men, were eating their packed lunches. Across the street from the construction site was an office building where a group of women were smoking outside during their break. One of the women whistled at him.

"Hey!" the smoker shouted with her raspy voice. "Come on over here, so I can talk to ya!"

Another said, "Aye, sexy! I won't bite!" The construction workers at the site witnessed this. They were shaking their heads in disgust during the outbursts.

"Look at that," one of the men said. "Pathetic. And all they want is what's in between your legs."

Dyanne was driving while talking to her best friend, Wanda, on her mobile phone. "So, you say this is a gathering for only the refined people?"

"That's right!" Wanda answered. "Only the best! Not like your ex. Or my ex."

"Which one? You had three of them!" She giggled.

"Oh, but you forgot the other two that

never happened!" She laughed aloud. "So are you coming out tonight?"

"Yeah, I'll be there. No telling who I might meet."

As Dyanne was driving, she noticed a couple of billboards and an advertisement on the transit bus with male models instead of the usual female models. She thought about it for only a few seconds, then shrugged it off.

♀
↓

Ron was eating his lunch in a booth at the diner down the street from his workplace. In the booth behind him was a group of four men having a conversation. These men were masculine. They talked like men, but they didn't say what men would normally say.

The first man discussed his issue. "So, this is only the third week of me knowing this chick, right? She took me to the mall a couple of times, gave me this nice watch." He flashed his gold watch. "She seemed like a nice gal. So, I agreed to go on this 'business trip' with her. But, only as a friend! I thought I made that part very clear!" He put his fork down with force. "Man, I had to straighten her out for acting all jealous when the other women there were talking to me! Fine women, too!" The men gasped in response to the woman's behavior. "And bruh, how come she tried to put the moves on me in the hotel room? Then, she gets all mad and calls me 'stuck up' for not giving up the pole! Women!"

Ron was shocked at what he heard from the next table! His lips read, "What the fuck?" but without sound.

A second man said, "See? They think that because they spend money on you, they own you! And you owe them something in return. Wrong!"

"Exactly!" the first man said. "I can afford my own! I don't need a woman for that! I am an independent man!"

Ron looked around the place, wondering if anyone else heard what he was hearing. The few people who were there showed no surprise.

↝

The man continued, "They got the game all twisted! Then, you have the ones who try to impress you with money, because they think that can make up for their bucket pussies!" Laughter erupted as the man went on. "This one woman was so wide, I don't know how she held a baby for a whole nine months! I mean wide, man!" He extended his arms, exaggerating the width of the woman's vagina. "I looked at her like, 'Get that thing away from me!' She thought I was supposed to get excited over <u>that</u>? A big ole bucket, man! I'm trying to have sex, not mop the floor! I ain't in no cleanin' mood!" He sipped his beverage while the guys were laughing hysterically. "I almost gave her some, until she pulled that trick. That was a complete turn-off!"

A third man at that same table spoke. "You all know the issues I had in the past. But my girlfriend, she just doesn't get it. I like her a lot, but the way she approaches me for sex is kind of like how my ex-girlfriend did." The men looked puzzled trying to figure out which girlfriend he was referring to. "You know... the one who raped me." Ron spit out his drink.

The third man continued. "Man, I almost had it with women! If this relationship doesn't work out, I might as well cross over to the gay dudes."

Ron called out to the waiter with food still on his plate. "Check, please! Waiter! I'm ready!"

Dyanne was standing at a service desk, signing up for a massage session at the parlor. She hesitated before signing her last name, then wrote her maiden name, Holmes.

The male secretary said, "Thank you, Ms. ...Holmes! Someone will be with you shortly."

When Dyanne turned towards the seating area, she was identified by an old high school buddy of hers, Denise Towers.

Also seated in the area was a Muslim couple. The wife was dressed in regular

〜

clothing while the husband was fully clothed in a burqa, including the cloth around his face. This was so his beauty would only be revealed to his wife, and to resist the attraction of another woman. Dyanne didn't notice this.

Denise inquired. "Holmes? Dyanne Holmes?"

"Um, yes," Dyanne responded. "Wait... Denise?"

"Yes, it's me! I haven't seen you in years! How have you been?"

"Good, Dee!" Dyanne said as she sat next to her. "How about you?"

"Girl, I'll be better once I finally get a massage. Sitting here wishing I had set up an appointment this time, instead of waiting up in here all day." She looked around. "You would think they had more men working back there! See, I come here often because of a back injury I had some months ago from a water skiing accident. I was skipping like a rock."

"Aw, poor thing! But, you're waiting on a

man to give you a massage? How long have you been waiting?"

"About forty-five minutes! And my back is killing me!" Someone's name was called other than Denise.

"Then, you need any help you can get, Dee! You had an injury! Why does it have to be a <u>man</u> massaging you?"

"I know, I know. It's not a sexual thing, but I just don't want a woman rubbing on me. It'll feel weird having a woman put her little hands on me like that." She lightly nudged Dyanne with her elbow and spoke quietly. "I'd rather wait for a masseur. I want strong hands rubbing against my body. And, I might want to talk with him. What am I going to talk about with a woman during a massage?" Dyanne was too surprised to answer. "And what could she be thinking about while massaging my back? I'm just not as comfortable with a masseuse."

Another name was called. Denise started to get bothered and irritated, but remained seated for a masseur. The man in the burqa rolled his eyes.

Dyanne was totally baffled by Denise's character. "Hmm. Well, I will be pampering myself today. Later, I have to pick up my kids from school, then take them to their dad's. And finally, more me time!" She had a sudden idea. "Hey, do you remember Wanda? We're hanging out tonight! You should come!"

"Oh, Wanda! Who could forget her? Sounds like fun! Let's exchange numbers."

As the two exchanged numbers, Dyanne's name was called for her session. Denise felt unhappy, because her name hadn't been called yet. The Muslim couple sat there, shaking their heads.

♀

As soon as Ron entered his office after taking his lunch break, a paper printed from his fax machine. He picked up the note which read:

"Ron, this is Raquel. Call my desk if you like what you see ;-)"

He looked down to the bottom of the page and his jaw dropped. Ron found several similar messages left for him while he was gone. Each fax included a picture of a nude body part of the sender. Ron took the stack of papers, sat at his desk, then dialed on the telephone.

Raquel's voice sounded through Ron's speaker phone. "Life Coverage. Raquel Matthews speaking..."

"Hello, Raquel. Are you busy?"

Viewable from outside of Ron's private office, Ron was walking to his window to close the blinds. Starting with Raquel, there was a sequence of women leaving in and out of his office having quickies with him.

After all of the trafficking was over, Ron reopened the blinds. He looked exhausted. He turned around and staggered back to his desk chair with his pants on backwards.

James and the mail clerks, who were three other men, were chit-chatting in the mailroom. One of the three mail clerks was Habib, an Arabic man who wore a burqa similar to the man who was at the massage parlor.

The mailroom door was slightly cracked open. The men were conversing loudly, believing that they were in private. It was a festive atmosphere with constant shouts. Ron peeked in without letting his presence be known.

One of the mail clerks talked about his relationship. "She is just the love of my life, bro! I got home last night and saw this big autographed poster of Dwayne Wade and an official NBA basketball with Lebron James' signature on it, like, damn that shit is beautiful!

"She knew exactly what to give me! Then later, she put it on me like a real woman! Baby had my leg shakin' like this-" He shook his leg like a jackhammer. "She knows just where my spot is!" There was an out roar among the group.

"Let me tell you about my girl," James said. "When we first got our house, I gave her a room to herself. I said, 'Baby, this is your woman cave. You can do whatever you like in this room.'

"See, you got to let your woman know that you trust her. Make her feel free and you'll be glad you did it!

"But what I didn't expect was, she put a padlock on that door! Six whole weeks go by and I'm thinking, 'She spends a lot of time in that room!'

"But, I didn't bother her about it. I wanted to show her that I still trust her. Even though we haven't been having sex. Most men I know wouldn't be able to handle this."

"I sure as hell wouldn't!" a coworker shouted adamantly.

"But! Just the other day, I came home wondering where she was. I hadn't heard from her. I tried calling, but her phone was off. I asked friends and family, but they hadn't heard from her, either.

"I started to worry and regretted giving her space. I was getting so mad, I wanted to make her sleep on the couch!

↜

"Then, I noticed a key on the dresser. It was small enough to fit into a padlock. I went to that room. I unlocked that door with the key. I opened it and there she was! Dressed in lingerie!

"The room got mirrors everywhere! Whips, handcuffs, costumes, a smoke machine, and every sexual device you can think of!

"Then, she tells me that she's been doing her Kegel's exercises to get her coochie nice and tight! Man, I damn near cried!" The men were jubilant after hearing James' story.

Ron walked in at the tail end of the discussion. "Hey fellas!"

The group dispersed. They weren't aware of Ron's presence until he spoke. They acted as if they didn't want to associate themselves with him.

All of them, including James, went back to doing their work with the mailings. There was a lack of eye contact.

"Why did you guys stop talking?" Ron

asked. "That was a good story! Well anyway, I got news of my own!" He stepped up as if he was about to make a big announcement. "Guys, I am having one of the best days of my life! If every dog has his day, then this one is mine!" He put his hands up to his mouth and barked like a dog. "Man, I just slept with every fine, sexy, single woman up in this place! Back to back, to back, to back! Tearing it up! Who's the man!" The men were not impressed.

"We already know," James said with no enthusiasm. "We heard…"

"What? You heard already? How in the hell? Well then, yeah. Uh, today's a good day." He looked over at Habib. "Habib, is that you? Man, why are you dressed like a ninja?"

Habib was appalled. "This is my culture! Do not insult my culture, Ron!"

"Uh, sorry, Habib. I don't mean any disrespect, but… Oh well, you guys enjoy the rest of your day." Ron left out of the mailroom.

↜

"It is confirmed," a mail clerk turned and said to James. "Your boy's a hoe."

ᗭhapter 6ᵗʰ

♧

he beautiful Dyanne finally made it to the beach. She wore a wide brim sun hat with ribbon. Dyanne's sheer cover-up over her two-piece bikini revealed her curvy figure, exposing her perfectly trimmed waistline and stomach. She looks good from head to toe and knows it.

Dyanne proceeded to the smoothie stand alongside the shore, but hesitated. "Why would I buy myself a drink?" she asked herself.

She put on her stylish yellow oversize sunglasses and looked around for the men in that area. She strutted across the sands where there was a row of chaises. Dyanne took a seat in the middle where she would be most noticeable. When she checked the time, it read 1:25pm.

〰

Dyanne said to herself, "Alright, Dy, you have ninety minutes."

A man passed by and barely looked her way. Then another. And then another, but this man perceptibly put a pep in his step as he walked within Dyanne's range. He trotted stiffly like a toy soldier. One man passed by, looked at her and smiled, but kept on walking. Dyanne was shocked!

Then, a family came and sat next to Dyanne. The couple had young kids who apparently started Spring Break already. They were recklessly shooting water guns and bouncing a beach ball around her. Their parents were doing nothing about it. The dad was hit square in the face with the ball, but just sat there like nothing happened.

Dyanne became agitated and headed back to the smoothie stand for a drink. On her way there, she saw a tall, oiled-up, muscular man wearing bikini shorts headed in her direction. He walked with much confidence. Across his six-pack abdominal muscles was a small tattoo that read, "Sexy Beast".

When the man got closer to her, she purposely stumbled in the sand, dropping her hat and sunglasses in the process. This was to get his attention. The man helped her gather her accessories, as a gentleman would.

"Thank you!" Dyanne said. "That was so clumsy of me!" She took a closer look at his muscles. "Wow! Look at your arms!"

Dyanne lightly touched the man's ripped biceps as he helped her up. He flinched back and got an attitude, because of the way she touched him. His pectoral muscles jumped as he raised his voice.

"Hey!" the cocky man shouted. "You can't just touch me like that! What are you trying to do?" Dyanne's head nodded up and down with each flex of his chest. "And I do have eyes! Hello!" He pointed to his eyes. "Up here, please!"

"What am I trying to do?" Dyanne asked. "What the hell <u>can</u> I do? You're, like, twice my size!"

"Yeah, you got a good look at that!" He pointed again. "Up here!"

"My head is at your chest, so where else am I supposed to look? You got your pecs bouncin' up and down right in my face, man! And why have on those tight ass trunks if you don't like being stared at? Seriously?"

"I dress this way because, yes, I like to feel sexy! It's my prerogative to dress the way I feel! But, that does not give you the right to disrespect me by staring at me! That's rude!" Dyanne was speechless. "Stumbling in the sand to get at me. How pathetic! Chicks will try anything!"

"Oh! Well, sorry for violating you, Mister Victim! With your bitch ass!" Dyanne stormed her way to the smoothie stand, kicking up sand.

Dyanne said to the bartender, "One Pina Coloda. Make it light, please. Don't want to be tipsy while picking up the kids." The bartender, who was obviously gay, prepared the drink. Dyanne looked at her watch which read 2:34pm.

"Damn!" Dyanne shouted. "It's been a full hour! Hey, what's up with the men around here? Is there some kind of gay convention going on?"

"What do you mean?" the bartender asked. "We're all perfectly normal."

"Well, I can't tell. Something is wrong! No offense to you."

"Here's your drink, Miss. Eight dollars." The transaction was made. "So, back to the men here... What is it that you expect from them?"

"Just men being... men!"

"And what does that mean? By whose standards are they supposed to live by?"

"It has never been this complicated before! Oh, pardon me. I am going through a divorce and it's been a long time since I've entered the dating scene. I didn't explain that part to you."

"Oh! Now I see. That is okay. Years?"

"Thirteen."

↘

"Yeah, that sounds tough to get over. The dating world has changed since then. Why not start a conversation with a guy?"

"Me start a conversation? No. Obviously, they don't want to be bothered anyway. Look at them." Dyanne pointed out pairs of men who were at the beach together.

Then, Dyanne spotted one man who sat comfortably in his beach chair by himself, reading a book. Dyanne watched as he ran his thumb across his tongue before turning each page of the book. His thumb glided across his mouth like a sailboat guided by the winds of the ocean.

He didn't drink from a plastic cup like everyone else. No, this handsome beau had his own glass of vanilla rum on ice. He stood out amongst others.

"Hey, wait a second," Dyanne said. "I wonder what he's reading." She left the smoothie stand to go to him. And the closer she got to him, the better he looked to her.

"Hi!" Dyanne said to the reader. "What's that you're reading?" she asked.

"The Lost Peninsula, by Gerard St. Clair," he said while raising his sunglasses above his eyesight.

"Hmm, a romance novel. Man and woman on the front cover. That is good. Sounds interesting." There was a slight pause. "My name's Dyanne. You just caught my attention, because I don't find too many guys reading books at the beach. At least not romance novels."

"Really? We're everywhere. You'll see plenty of us if you come around here more often." He reached for a handshake.

"Darvin Martel," he said, "I'm part of a book club." She shook his hand. "We meet up at this beach throughout the week around this time. Are you reading anything now?"

Dyanne laughed. "I haven't picked up a novel in a long time. Only children's books. That's because I run a daycare center."

"That's good!"

"I'm on a short vacation right now. So, how good is Gerard St. Clair?"

↬

"Not just good, but one of the best writers, in my opinion. I am loving this book right now!" He flipped to an illustration within the book. "See, the lost peninsula represents Michael, the main character, and his lack of a sex drive. He finds it when he travels to a distant land where he falls for Rebbecca. But, he is also in love with Marianne and Zina. It's a good book!"

"Peninsula, penis..." Dyanne said. "Yeah, I get it. So, not only are you reading a romance novel, but the main character is a man. Okay... Well, I have to go get my children from school. Hopefully, I'll see you again soon."

"Oh? Kids? That's nice. What are their ages?"

"My son is thirteen and my daughter is eight."

"It is so good to see a woman who takes care of her children. Owning up to her responsibilities."

"Huh? We're everywhere!"

"Well, I'll be here tomorrow. Hope to see

you again soon, too!"

As Dyanne left, the bartender from the smoothie stand gave her a salute from a distance. She gave one back.

Ron stepped out of his office, and there waiting was Luann. Launn's personality was exactly the same as it was the previous days. Same big smile.

Luann startled Ron. "Mr. Long!"

"Whoa, uh, hey Luann."

"How is your day?"

"Luann, it is quite productive."

"I am so glad to hear that! Wow! If you're happy, then I'm happy!"

"Good for... you, Luann. I must be-"

"Your boss wants to see you."

"Uh, any idea why?"

"Nope! She said right away."

"Alrighty then."

Ron stepped in a slow motion towards his boss's office. When he walked by, he caught eyes with some of the women whom he had sexual relations with earlier that day. As they smiled and gave him flirtatious gestures, the men of the office gave him the look of shame. They shook their heads at him.

Ron made it to the door of Harriet Harland, the head manager of the facility. She is not considerably attractive and is old enough to retire. Ron took a deep breath before opening the door. He entered inside where Harriet was sitting behind her desk.

"Sit your sexy ass down!" Harriet commanded.

Ron immediately sat down as he was told. He looked around the office avoiding eye contact with Harriet. He could tell when she was upset by the way she heaved through her nostrils.

"Mr. Long!" shouted Harriet, followed by a deep breath.

"Yes! Ma'am?"

"I hear you've been running a freak show in my office. Is that correct?"

"I- I'm not sure exactly what you mean by that, Ms. Harland."

"Oh yes you do! I've been working for this company for nearly fifty years. I'm still not ready to retire! You know why? Because none of the jackasses under me are good enough to replace me!" She inhaled hard. "You are one of those jackasses! You and your colleagues are living, breathing, failed insurance policies! How ironic it is for a company that covers people in case of calamities to have no replacement for their own superior leader!"

"Gee, Harriet, I didn't know you considered me as a possible successor at all. I never thought about replacing you. Now I'm even more regretful for ruining things."

"Don't act all sentimental on me, you jerk! You did what you wanted to do! I'm going to have to take action against your slutty behavior!"

"Hold on! I didn't go to those women and jerk off! They came to me and I gave them what they wanted! It was consensual!" He mentioned the faxes that were sent to his office. "I got the papers to prove it! They should be in here, too! Why single me out?"

"Provocative clothing is a distraction and can fall under the category of sexual harassment!"

"Her ass meant what?"

"What? How do you expect women to react with the way you flaunt yourself in that provocative clothing?"

"How are my clothes provoking these women? What's that all about?"

"Your clothes are too tight! I can see your triceps through your shirt! That is inappropriate!"

"Huh? Triceps? And those women's blouses aren't tight? I've had nipples pointing at me all day!"

"Nipples? So, you think I'm going to shut down this whole facility because of you? You can't blame women for being women!" She points at Ron. "Mr. Long, you are the common denominator! You knew this would happen. Stop playing dumb!"

"How are you blaming me? This is some

sexist bullshit! I can't believe this!"

"So what now? A discrimination lawsuit? I'd like to see you try."

"Look, I can work anywhere. I'm not intimidated."

"You're talking about quitting? I didn't even specify what disciplinary actions I was going to take! Loser!"

"I'm listening..."

"...We can avoid all of this, of course. Look under the desk."

Ron was suspicious. "You know, I believe in going by the book. That is the only way to make things go smoothly-"

"No, you fool! It's not what you think, silly. Take a look..."

Ron looked under Ms. Harland's desk, then popped right back up immediately. "I'll take the disciplinary actions, please!"

↝

Chapter 7th

*L*ate in the afternoon, Luann arrived home from work. Luann's Mom was there watching classic black and white movies, again.

Luann greeted her mother. "Mom, I'm home!" Luann's mom grunted. "Are you feeling better today, Mother?"

"Chocolate cake! I want my German chocolate cake!"

"Now you want chocolate cake? I don't know what to do to please you, mom. First you wanted cheesecake, then you wanted red velvet, and now you want chocolate cake!"

"Luann! Did you forget again? Can't you remember to get what I tell you to get?"

"Okay mom, I'm going to do what I should have done a long time ago." Luann fetched a pen and a notepad, then brought it to her mother. "Here, write down what you want me to bring, so I won't forget it the next time I come back in. How is that?"

Luann's mom put on her bifocal lens glasses that were hanging from the link around her neck. She grabbed the pen and notepad, then she wrote with her <u>fist</u> in big letters. She checked her handwriting half way through, then proceeded to the finish. She proofread her message after she finished and handed it to Luann. It read:

"A MAN!"

Luann became angry. "Mom! Why are you so mean to me? I am tired of this! I will get a man when I am ready!"

"You can't get a man!" her mother said. "No man wants you! Painting houses pink!"

"I told you! I painted the house purple a year ago! You haven't seen it, because you never go outside, Ma!"

"I don't want to see my house pink! All

↩

that pink."

"The! House! Is! Purple!"

"No man wants a pink house!"

"SHUT UP! I HAVE TRIED! OH, I'VE TRIED! BUT, I HAD ENOUGH OF YOUR EVIL COMMENTS! I CAN'T TAKE IT ANYMORE! EVERYDAY YOU WATCH THOSE OLD MOVIES OVER AND OVER AGAIN!

"YOU WON'T TAKE YOUR MEDICATION! THIS ENTIRE HOUSE SMELLS LIKE ASS CRACK! I CAN'T EVEN USE THE WASHING MACHINE, BECAUSE IT MAKES MY CLOTHES SMELL LIKE ASS CRACK! NO MAN WANTS TO SMELL ASS CRACK! And you know what? I DO REMEMBER! I REMEMBER EVERYTHING!"

"...Damn pink house."

Luann yelled, "Argh! ...Mom, it's time for your bath." Luann began to roll her mom's wheelchair where she sat. She headed for the bathroom.

Luann's mom panicked. "No! You're trying to drown me!"

ↆ

"Mom! We go through this every time! You need to get washed up!"

Luann made it to the bathroom door, but her mom held still against the door frame. Luann tried to move her mom's stiffened arms so she could get her through the door and into the bathroom.

Luann demanded, "Stop...holding...back!"

Her mother screamed, "No! I don't want a bath!"

Luann finally got her mother through the door. The shower head is detachable and can be used as hand-held sprayer. The tub has a sling over it for bathing the disabled.

"Look!" Luann yelled. "I won't plug the drain! The water will not fill up! You can't drown that way!"

"You'll never get me in there!"

Luann ran the water and prepared the sling, so she could sit her mom in it to bathe her. But, her mom reached around her, snatched the detachable shower head off of the clamp, and sprayed her with warm water!

↜

Luann screamed! She escaped after slipping and sliding across the bathroom floor.

Her mom laughed deviously. "I got you now! Dance! Dance!"

♀

In Ron's apartment, he and his children, Ronald III and Marla, were playing a board game. They played on the dining room table with the TV playing across the room. Airing on the television station was a music video.

"I'm about to win again!" Marla sang.

Ronald III replied, "Only if Dad lets you win again! I won't let you."

"Sometimes, you should let the ladies have their way," his dad, Ron, said. "You'll learn that when you get a bit older, son. Speaking of which, I want to have a talk with you after this game. Nothing bad, just a man talk." He told Marla, "Sweetie, you can just sit here and watch the..."

As Ron turned towards the television, he had to do a double-take. There was a raunchy music video playing with women popping champagne bottles on men who were dancing around shirtless. One female rapper threw up a handful of money and "let it rain" on two of the male models who were dancing closely together.

"What the hell is this?" Ron asked while investigating. "Change the channel!"

Ronald III plead, "Come on, Dad! That's one of hottest songs out right now! 'Check the Fine Print'. I just like the beat. Guess what it's about..." The video made it obvious that the song was referring to looking at a man's crotch or "dick print" in his shorts.

Ron watched, then became furious! "They're talking about his dick print? Oh hell no! Cover your eyes, Marla! Ronnie, stop bobbing your head!" Ron snatched the remote control with fierce and turned the TV completely off.

Ronald III whined, "Aw, Dad! That wasn't as bad as Lil' Big-Boned, with her 'Swing It, Swing It' video!"

"Who the hell is that?" Ron asked. "Look, when they tell you to throw your hands in the air and stuff like that, you don't do it! Only do what I say! Daddy says! 'F' Simon!" He tossed the remote. "We'll finish this game later, kids. Ronnie, come with me. Marla, turn on the video game. You can play it until we get back and wait for Granddad."

Ron and his son went into the bedroom. Ron dropped a big, heavy cardboard box onto his bed. Ronald III looked curious. The box was taped up and read: "Ron's Library; DO NOT OPEN!!"

Ronald III asked, "Dad, what's in the box?"

Ron took out a blade. He cut the tape and opened the box. Inside were stacks of video cassettes. These cassettes are copies with handwriting on the sticker labels and no covers.

"These are called video cassettes," Ron said. "They were popular before DVDs came out. You can fit more than one movie into each of these."

"Whoa!"

"Yes. And this collection I have here is very special. Now, your mom told me that your school gave you a Sex Education class."

"Uh, yes."

"Well, that stuff never helped me. I'm going to show you how it really is." He powered on the electronics. "When you find that first dame, hopefully your wife, I don't want you confused from that silly class and those stupid music videos. This is how a man is supposed to take care of business."

Ron located a cassette that read: "School of Hard Knockin' the Boots, Volume 182 & 184." For some odd reason, Ron thought it was a good idea to use this tape as a "walk-through".

He continued. "This video here is an all-time classic series and my personal favorite. I used to have it set precisely at my favorite- I meant, most informative- scene, but I'm not sure if I left it there last time." He pointed above the TV. "On top of the television is a video cassette recorder. VCR for short. You can record from the TV and even another cassette."

"Wow! That is so cool, Dad! Why did they stop making these?"

Ron popped in the tape and handled the remote. He sat next to Ronald III, who was sitting on the bed directly in front of the television. Ron pressed play. The glow of the TV screen shined upon them like the sun rising above the horizon.

Ron said, "Okay, here is the man. He's going to show how it's done... Now here comes... Oh, there's another man... I don't remember this part. What the?...What the?"

Ronald III asked, "Why does it look so...gritty? Ew, Dad! They're kissing! Gross!"

"Hey! What the hell is this?"

"Yuck! He's about to... Dad, I don't want to see this!" Ron hastily pushed Fast Forward on the remote. "Ugh! Dad, I can still see it! He's just doing it faster! Why don't you just skip the scene?"

"I can't! It's just a tape player! Cover your eyes, boy!"

Ron put his hand over his son's eyes. There was a knocking on the bedroom door. This startled Ron! He reacted like a teen who was caught watching porn. He unplugged all of the electronics from the wall.

Marla called out from the other side of the door. "Are you guys okay in there? Do you need help?"

"No, honey!" Ron shouted frantically. "We're okay! Go back to the video game, sweetheart!"

"Okay, Daddy! Have a safe man talk!"

Ron explained to Ronald III, "I don't know how, but your mother must have sabotaged my tape! I swear I don't remember that crap! And she must have somehow taped the box back exactly the way I had it! I don't watch or buy porn like this!" He put his hands on his son's shoulders. "Are you okay, son? I didn't mean to traumatize-"

"It's cool, Dad," Ronald III said. "I got a confession."

"A confession!" Ron almost lost his cool

again, but gathered himself. "Wait. Sorry for yelling at you that way, son. I want you to know that you can talk to me about anything. Okay? Just tell me what it is and remember that I love you still. Even though I may not agree-"

"Dad! I watch porn on my computer! That is my confession!"

"Oh. Thank goodness."

"So, I know how they always include those scenes. Women like that for some reason."

"Really?"

"Yeah, don't you see it everywhere?"

"I guess so..."

"This is nothing new to me, Dad. Then, they have the guys taking turns going down on the woman. Same ole, same ole."

"Wait! What are you doing watching this filth behind our backs? If they're showing scenes like the one your mother put on my tape, then don't watch it!" He thought for a second, then snapped his fingers. "I know what to do! I'll let your Granddad set you straight! He's from the old school! He won Man of the Year for Veterans! Your Granddad is a man's man!"

Outside of the apartment building where Ron resided, a van drove up. It has many bumper stickers pertaining to war and the Marines. Exiting the van was Colonel Ronald Long Sr., a retired veteran and Ron's father. He wore a dog tag, a whistle, and combat boots with his pants tucked in them.

As he marched across the parking lot, he heard a heavy bass sound coming from a distant vehicle's stereo system. This caused him to halt and observe the premises. The loud car arrived and the driver parked across from Col. Long's van. The driver got out and hit his alarm switch. Col. Long started walking again, but then, the driver's car suddenly backfired!

Col. Long ran and jumped behind his van, yelling, "Under fire! Under fire!"

He waited. He peeked around his van and saw the driver of the loud car calmly walking to the apartment building. When the driver made it through the doors, Col. Long came from behind the van and marched again.

Ron and the kids were playing the video game as Col. Long blew his whistle from the other side of the door in order to be let in. Marla went to the door and opened it.

"A ten hut!" Col. Long shouted.

Marla cheered, "Granddad!"

"Come on in, Dad," Ron said.

Col. Long hugged Marla. "What kind of man has his little girl opening doors to let people in?"

"We knew it was you, she was waiting on you, and I don't respond to whistles anymore. Hello to you, too, Pop."

Col. Long addressed Ronald III. "Ron three! Front and center! Straighten your back, boy! Stop slouching! Give your Grandpa a handshake!" He shook his hand. "Good firm shake, grandson! You've been working on your grip!"

"You have no idea, sir," Ronald III said.

"Not funny, Ronnie," said Ron. "Colonel Dad, I was hoping you would give your grandson a lesson in old school manhood, if you know what I mean. He's at that age."

"Hmm, I see..." Colonel Long responded. "Gentlemen! Come with me! That means you too, Ron." Ron, his father, and his son stepped outside onto the balcony through the sliding screen door.

"Ron three!" Col. Long shouted. "Look at your father!" He looked at Ron. "This is an example of what not to be like!"

"Hey!" yelled Ron in his resentment.

"I'll show you how real men treated women in the old school! Our way was the right way! Ron three!"

"Yes sir!" Ronald III responded.

"You're out with a lady. There is a door in front of you. What do you do?"

"Uh, go through the door, sir."

"No! You stand there until she opens the door for you!"

Ron yelled out, "What?"

Col. Long continued. "Who orders their

ↄↄ

meal first?"

Ronald III asked, "The one who knows what they want? Sir?"

"Wrong again! She orders first! Why? Because, she is supposed to take charge!" He tapped his grandson's chest. "Stay in a man's place, boy! And remember, the woman always pays the bill!"

"Are you serious?" Ron asked. "As good as some of that sounds, there is no way in hell a woman will go for that!"

"You're the one to talk! I've been married to your mother for over thirty-five years! How is your marriage going?"

"Dad. This is not the talk that I had in mind. You're teaching my son how to be a pimp!"

"You said teach the boy the old school and that's what I am doing! Now..." Again, he faced Ronald III. "Don't give it up on the first night! Let her know you're a gentleman by making her wait!"

"This is ridiculous, Pops! Alright, my mistake. Ronnie is not ready for this talk, yet." He opened the screen door back to the apartment. "I'll pick up from where we're leaving off for another time. It's time for you kids to go stay at your grandparents'." He said to Col. Long, "After you, sir..."

When Col. Long exited, Ron cleverly handed Ronald III a pack of firecrackers. They left the porch together.

Chapter 8ᵗʰ

*I*nside of a women's clothing store, Dyanne stepped out of the dressing room. She was gorgeous in a nicely-fitted black dress for the evening party she was going to attend afterward with her friends. She went to the saleslady and posed.

"How do I look?" Dyanne asked.

"It fits well," the saleslady said. "That's a nice dress."

Dyanne was not convinced and quite disappointed by her answer. She tried on another dress, but the saleslady still avoided showing much enthusiasm. This happened two more times and Dyanne was annoyed.

"Look, I'm trying to get a second opinion here," Dyanne said. "Help a sister out."

"You should get what makes you feel good," the saleslady said. "It shouldn't matter what my opinion is." Dyanne frowned at her disgracefully. "Actually, Miss, you should get a man's opinion instead."

Dyanne asked her, "If you don't have an eye for fashion, then what are you doing working here?" She huffed. "Just give me this dress. You really earned your commission." She spoke in a sarcastic tone.

After Dyanne left the clothing store, she traveled down the main aisle of the shopping mall. She spotted a men's store that specialized in intimate apparel. The name of the store was Victor's Secret. It had huge posters of attractive men dressed in night clothes on the glass windows. Dyanne walked in that direction until she realized that the only customers in there were men.

One of the customers was the fully-clothed Muslim husband from earlier at the massage parlor. He was facing away from Dyanne. He held up a pair of tight, silk

ⵎ

underwear. Then, he put the underwear against his fully clothed waist, sizing it up on himself. Again, Dyanne didn't notice him.

Dyanne thought to herself, "Victor's? This is weird."

Dyanne continued down the main aisle. She came across the bookstore and saw Darvin Martel, the reader who was lounging at the beach earlier. She went inside.

Dyanne smiled at Darvin. "I swear I'm not stalking you."

Darvin laughed. "Hi, Dyanne! Didn't expect to see you here! Kid's section is two rows down."

"Ha! You got jokes. What a coincidence seeing you here! I was buying an outfit for girls' night out with my friends..." She thought for a second. "Hey! I need your opinion! Come to this store with me, will you? I want you to tell me what you think about these dresses."

"Sure, I got time."

Dyanne took Darvin by the hand, pulling

him out of the bookstore until they arrived at the women's clothing store. Inside, Dyanne came out of the dressing room wearing one of the outfits she tried on before.

"What do you think?" she asked Darvin.

"Wow," Darvin said in a dry tone. "It looks nice on you."

"Better than the other one?"

"They both look nice. I like this one better."

"Then, I'll go with this one. You know... I really can't tell with you."

"Tell what?"

"It's like you're holding back." Darvin was clueless. "You say the dresses look good on me, but you won't say that I look good <u>in</u> the dresses. If something is on your mind, then you should say it. You're too bashful. Loosen up!"

"Well, I didn't want to act too hysterical about how you looked in those dresses. Some women get the 'big head' and I didn't want to contribute to the female ego. You

࿔

know..."

"Ego? What ego? You think I'm a narcissist?"

"No, I'm just saying-"

"You said enough. You know what? I'll be on my way. Thanks for your help." Dyanne purchased the outfit that she had just tried on. Apparently, she was upset. After the purchase, she walked away without speaking another word. Darvin showed regret.

♀

Ron was on the phone with his brother, Aaron. "All I can say is, Dad has lost his mind! That military stuff just took him to a whole new level of crazy! I need a drink."

"Me too," Aaron said. "Let's get there before twelve, so we can get in free."

"Free before twelve? Cool! They finally got Guy's Night Out!"

"Every night is Guy's Night Out when we go out, bro. So... you're still single, right?"

"You bet! Oh, and I got some things to tell you! What a day I'm having!"

"Save it for the bar, big bro. We're going to have a good talk. You've been out of the game for far too long, so I might need to give you a refresher course."

"Oh really? You just don't know, player! See you there!"

"Later." They ended their call.

In the luxurious ballroom of a famous hotel, Dyanne sat alone at the bar. She was looking lovely in the black dress that she bought earlier. A couple sat a few stools down from her to the left. Another woman sat alone a few stools down from her to the right. She called her best friend on her cellphone.

"Wanda!" Dyanne shouted. "What is taking you so long? I've been here for fifteen minutes! Where are you?"

"I'll be there in a minute!" Wanda responded. "Just chill. Where's our old friend?"

"Denise hasn't gotten here yet, either. You girls are slow!"

↝

"I'm on my way! What do the guys look like over there?"

Dyanne spotted two men at a table. One of them she found to be very attractive. He looked back at her for a split second, then whispered to his buddy sitting across from him.

"Hold on, Wanda," Dyanne said. "I think I got a fish. A hot one at that! I'll see you when you get here."

Wanda replied, "Get 'em, wild cat! Meow!"

Dyanne hung up the phone and glanced at the table where the two men were seated. The stunning man smiled and whispered to his buddy again. Then, his friend left the table and went to the restroom. Dyanne put her phone in her purse and took out her pocket-sized mirror. She checked herself for imperfections, then put the mirror back into her purse.

The stunning man just sat there, looking in her direction, but not directly at her. Then, he looked away. Dyanne did the same thing; looked in his direction, but not at him, and then looked away.

Minutes went by and there was no interaction between them. Finally, the stunning man's buddy came back. They spoke to each other, but without whispering this time. Every now and then, their eyes would peek toward Dyanne.

"... must be lesbian..." the buddy said.

The stunning man responded, "Right!"

The two men laughed. Dyanne heard this and knew that they were referring to her. This made her feel uncomfortable.

Dyanne quietly said to herself, "Did he just say what I think he said?"

Outside of the nightclub entrance, women were lined up alongside the wall to get inside. Men were walking straight in. When Ron walked by the women, a few of them flirted. He smiled and went inside the nightclub with no hassle.

Aaron was seated at the bar. He looked up and saw Ron approaching him. The two greeted each other and embraced.

〜

"Glad you made it!" Aaron said, with a peck to Ron's cheek. "I thought you were going to miss the deadline."

"Nah, I can't miss out on a deal," Ron said, wiping his cheek.

"So, what's this news you got? What's going on with you?"

"Do you remember when we were kids and I used to let you read my Superman comic books?"

"Yep."

"Well, I feel like I stepped into Bizarro World. But, as Bizarro!"

"Break it down, as only you can, Ron."

"Check this out, bro. In our world, Bizarro is screwed up. He's not perfect. His 'S' is on backwards. Just screwed up, thoroughly!" Aaron was attentive. "When he came to this world, he was considered a villain. But as it turned out, he was just at the wrong place at the wrong time. He has a world of his own! And in that world, he is the shit!" He leaned forward to his brother's ear. "See, when I was going through all of that stuff before today, that was the typical world. But, I'm thee shit right now!" He lifted his arms. "Bizarro: Chick Magnet! They can't get enough of me!

"And a lot of these guys sound like wimps, too!"

"Bro, I was thinking the same thing!" Aaron said. "These guys have no class, game, or intermission. Get it? Intermission?"

"Deep! Break that down for me, player! Wait, first let's order a round."

"Order a round? Okay, the refresher course is now in effect. Turn your seat a little and get your profile on. One of these ladies will be glad to buy you a drink."

"Damn! You got it like that? Man, you always were able to get one up on me!"

Right when Ron looked around, his eyes met with a pretty woman in orange. She whispered something to the bartender. The bartender headed Ron's way with a drink.

He passed Ron the drink. "Courtesy of the lady in orange."

〜

Ron yelled across the bar to the lady, "Thanks, baby!" He turned to Aaron. "Bro! You were right!"

This sexy lady in orange went by the name, Serena Kyle. She has the looks of a cover model, but goes overboard with her styles. Her hair was whipped like a soft-served ice cream sundae of many flavors, sensitive to the touch. Her technicolor garments virtually illuminated in the shadows, leaving motion streaks as she pranced across the aphotic stretch. The high and flashy stiletto heels she wore on her feet justified her prideful claim of being an inch short of six feet in height. She was basically walking on her toenails. And her glistening gold tooth gave her smile the same effect as a sunken treasure chest deep within the ocean, waiting to be discovered by an acclaimed explorer.

She stepped up to Ron smoothly. "Hey baby, my name is Serena Kyle. They call me Queen Bees-ness."

Ron laughed. "That's so cute! Your name

is like Cat Woman's. We were just talking about comic books! Cool, so, what is your occupation, Ms. Kyle?"

"I am the CEO of 'Off the Chain, Nigga!! Entertainment'. I got hot artists lined up, getting their shoes shined up. Ain't nothing whack, I can prove that in my pink Cadillac."

Serena showed off her car keys to prove that she has a Cadillac. As Serena ranted, she checked out Ron's physique without having much eye contact. Of course, Ron didn't mind it at all. Serena flicked out her business card. The logo had a Black male slave breaking his shackles apart.

"Here's my card, baby," Serena said. "Call up that number and you'll see why they call me Queen Bees-ness."

"Well aren't you special!" Ron responded. "Got the keys to prove it, huh? I see you like to rhyme, too. That's... different. And so is this name and logo. It's off the chain!"

"I'm full of surprises, sexy man." Serena walked off, switching her butt with a smile.

↝

Ron checked out her booty as she walked away. "Alright, with yo fine self! Thanks for the drink!"

Aaron was disgusted. "That woman must think you're a hoe or something. 'I'm full of surprises'. More like full of shit. Do you want me to twat-block chicks like her?"

"Twat-block?" Ron asked. "Hell naw! Did you see the rack on that with the booty to match?"

"Are you serious? Then, let me start my break-down of inter-mission."

"After today's success, I think I've done well on my own! I'm the one with the drink! Where's yours?" He chuckled at his brother. "Look, your inter-mission causes dry mouth!" He let out a hearty laugh. "And no telling what other side effects!" He took a gulp of his drink. "Man, where did you get that 'twat-block' talk from, anyway? You sound crazy."

Aaron replied, "While you laugh, she doesn't even know your name. While you laugh, she doesn't know anything about you. And while you're still grinning, she's giving out her number to another dude."

After Aaron said this, Ron stopped laughing and grinning. And as Aaron said, Serena was showing her "Bees-ness card" to another man. Ron was a little surprised by her behavior. He took another gulp of his drink.

Ron barely responded. "Well, uh...Hmm... Enough about her. Even good days like this has its bad news. I was suspended for a week without pay."

"Suspended? For what?"

"Having too much of a good time."

ↄ

Chapter 9ᵗʰ   🐿

At the hotel ballroom, Dyanne was dozing off at the bar where she had been sitting. Suddenly, both Wanda and Denise showed up at the party together.

"Dyanne!" Wanda shouted. "Hey, girl! We see you dozing off!"

Dyanne said abruptly, "I'm not sleep. Hey, you two were together?"

"We ran into each other in the lobby. Got caught up on our lives. That's what took us so long."

Denise said, "Yeah, Wanda told me a lot."

Dyanne looked at Wanda. "I bet she did."

"Well anyway," Wanda said, "check out the eye candy in here! And they all got their own! Let's sit at a table, so we can get a better view."

The ladies moved away from the bar area to get seated at a table. The setting was elegant. Each table was decorated with extravagant tableware and utensils in place, with a centerpiece dressing the middle.

Denise looked around. "Lord have mercy! Dy, you didn't get on any of these fine specimen, yet?"

"Naw, they've been acting a bit strange," Dyanne said. "Look on the dance floor. They dance in groups!" They observed a group of four men dancing together in a circle.

"So what?" Wanda responded. "Just go over there and yank one of them. You have been out of the game for too long, Dy."

"But, look at that! They're dancing with each other!" She pinpointed people on the dance floor. "Other than those few couples, this looks like a party for gay men."

"Gay men? They're not even touching! They just want to dance, that's all. If you had your butt out there, maybe they would be dancing with you!"

"I'm sorry, but that does not look

welcoming at all. Nor does it look sexy. Let's order some food."

"That sounds good!" Denise said. "I'm ready to eat!"

Later, their small meals were placed on the table. The DJ played a song that brought back memories of their younger days.

Wanda laughed out, "Oh snap! Dyanne, do you remember back in the seventh grade when we had that school dance? You really liked that one boy. I think his name was Stephen!" Dyanne rolled her eyes at Wanda. "Yeah, that's it!"

Wanda asked Denise, "Do you remember that, Dee? So, Dyanne puts on these white lace stockings to go with her black pleather mini skirt!" She laughed. "She had those itty bitty legs, too! And you know they didn't make stockings like that for little girls! She probably stole them from her momma or something!" She laughed even harder. "'Cause, I know damn well they didn't let her go outside with that on! Girl, those stockings were baggy as hell!"

"Oh yeah!" Denise said. "I do remember that! I didn't want to say anything about it, but yeah, that was funny."

"It looked like she ran through a bunch of spider webs! Those stockings fitted her like Hammer pants!"

"Alright now," Dyanne said, "that was long ago. Let's be mature."

"Ooooh!"

Denise interrupted, "Come on, Dyanne. It's all in love."

"Right, don't be that way," Wanda said. "Please! Hammer! Don't hurt me! Ha, ha! You should've seen yourself doing the Running Man with those on!"

Dyanne replied, "And what about all the lil' polka dot-wearing boys you had fighting over you back then? Rolling on the ground at the fight corner, looking like a game of craps." Denise giggled.

"Aye, that's what's up!" Wanda said. "I had it like that! Don't hate now!"

"Who's hating? You sure are acting

funny, Wanda. First, you invite me to a party full of men who apparently don't like women. Then, you goof around while I wait. And now, you insult me on some seventh grade garbage? How immature."

"Look, I know separating from your husband can be hard on you, but I'm just trying to get you to laugh at life. Don't be so serious! You're in a place full of sexy, distinguished men! Have at it!"

Dyanne stared at Wanda suspiciously. Then, a well-groomed muscular man walked by.

"Whoa!" shouted Denise. "Look at him! Check out his pecs! Damn!"

"Those aren't real," Wanda said.

Dyanne was astonished! "What? Not real?"

"You can tell by his upper chest. That is too much thickness on his collar bone. They over-did it." The ladies observed. "And look at his shoulders. They're too small for a chest that size. He's not proportioned well at all."

"You're right!" Denise said. "I bet that job cost a fortune, too!"

Dyanne gasped. "Implants? That is lazy. He'd rather spend money on implants than exercise. He didn't need to do all of that to himself, he's cute enough."

"Oh, I didn't even look at his face."

Ron and Aaron were still sitting at the bar in the nightclub. Ron was a bit tipsy.

"So, what are you going to do with this time off?" Aaron asked.

"I don't know," Ron said. "I'm thinking about applying elsewhere, but I can already imagine..." Ron, in his nearly-drunken state, imagined himself being interviewed at an office for a new job.

The interviewer gave his evaluation. "So, Mr. Long, you were Lead Supervisor of the Auto Claims department. Eight years on the job. Impressive!

"We pay twice more than what your old job did. You would like it here! We have month-long vacations, two raises a year, whether you've done well or not. Oh, and don't worry about being here on time. We'll work with you on that.

"Now, let's take a look at your work record..." He flipped through a stack of papers. "Screwed a lot of people on their claims. That's good news!" He flipped through a few more sheets. "Screwed a lot of women who worked at the job? Not good news!

"Well, Mr. Long, there are more beautiful young women working here than at your old job.

"The temptation may be too much for you to handle. And I can't ignore what you've done at that other place. All I can offer for you is... look under the desk." Said with a devious grin.

Ron snapped out of his dream. "As a matter of fact, that is out of the question! I'm going to wrap my head around what's been going on lately."

Aaron said, "You might want to cut it with the drinks, bro. You don't have a designated driver. Unless, you want to leave here in a pink Cadillac."

"I won't leave my ride here. And no more drinks for me. I don't care who's buying."

"With that being said, bro, it's time for me to head out. I got work in the morning."

"I'll head outside with you."

Back inside the hotel ballroom, the ladies were finished with their small meals. Wanda took notice of an attractive man in their line of view.

Wanda alerted Dyanne. "Dy! Ten o' clock!" Dyanne was confused. "Dang, girl! Dude in the gray slacks! Check the print!"

Dyanne asked, "Wanda, did you drink on your way here?"

But, Denise stated, "I'm sober, and he looks good to me."

"Thank you, Dee!" Wanda responded. "Dyanne is trippin'!"

"How am I trippin'?" Dyanne asked.

"Dy, when was the last time you approached a man? Besides your hubby?"

〜

"This afternoon, for your information. But really, it wasn't so much that I was 'approaching' him. I saw him reading a book at the beach and I wondered what he was reading about."

"Ooo! Was it one of those romance novels?"

"Wow, how did you guess? It actually was."

Denise yelled, "Freak!"

"Who?" Dyanne asked. "Darvin? Nah, I don't think he's that type at all."

Wanda said, "I never met him and I already know he is! He's got Freak all over him! Nothing would make that man more happier than a wet cooch!"

Dyanne shook her head. "Wanda, Wanda, Wanda."

"What, what, what? This man was on the beach reading a sexy book! Come on, now, if that ain't a sign, I don't know what is. Are you blind?"

"You never even met the guy!"

"You better be glad I <u>wasn't</u> around,

'cause I would already be hittin' it by now." Denise cosigned with Wanda.

"Ladies!" Dyanne responded. "Why are you so quick to judge? I just met him! Yes he's a man and all, but he didn't even try to come on to me!"

Wanda was disappointed. "Damn, Dy. Tell me you're just playing naive. Please tell me!" She leaned closer to Dyanne. "Those quiet, innocent types are thee biggest freaks! They have so much to hide! You need to woman up and stop being a sissy!"

"What the hell did you just say to me?"

"I'm telling you the real! Grow some pubic hairs and grab that ass!"

"Oh no you didn't!"

"Dyanne, you are my best friend. I'm only telling you based on my experiences. And you know I've had experiences. Okay, you see the man in the gray slacks, right?"

"Yes I see the man in the gray slacks. What?"

"Go talk to him!"

"About what? How's his food? Nice

slacks? Is he drunk yet? What the hell am I supposed to say?"

"It's been that long, Dy?" Denise asked.

Wanda told Dyanne, "Homegirl, just ask him what type of business he's in. Talk about this place and ask if he's been to better places. Just have fun!"

Then, Dyanne asked, "So, I am to pretend that I'm interested in other things besides his good looks? Even though I really don't care about anything else? Smile and try not to make it look fake?"

"Exactly!"

Dyanne took another look at the man in gray slacks. He was having a conversation with his friends. Dyanne was too nervous and needed an excuse not to go to that booth.

"He's talking to his friends," Dyanne said. "Am I to interrupt them? He might think that is rude-"

"Do you want me to go with you?" Wanda asked. "I'll occupy his friends for you. You know I got the gift of gab. Come on!" Wanda pulled Dyanne's arm, but Dyanne snatched it back.

"No, wait! We're here as friends! We haven't been together in years! Tonight is about us, not them! I'm not going to talk it up with those guys and leave Denise behind!"

But, Denise said, "Go ahead, I'm good." Then, two women joined the table where the man in the gray slacks and his friends were seated.

Wanda became frustrated. "See, Dyanne? Look at that! You just let those other chicks creep right on in! Did you see that? Dick just gone. You let it fly right on out the window!"

Chapter 10th

Ron was outside of the nightclub after spending time with his younger brother, Aaron. He leaned slightly against Serena Kyle's pink car, waiting for her as she left from the club.

Serena cried out, "Oh! Baby!" She hurried to the car and moved Ron out of the way to inspect her car for damages. "My man, please watch the paint! I just got it waxed, baby!"

"You're here by yourself?" Ron asked. "It's too dangerous for a sexy woman like you to be out here alone like this."

"Nobody's going to harm this body. I'm armed. Wanna frisk me?"

"Yeah, we can do that, but what about those other guys you were talking with?"

"Aw baby, that was just Bees-ness."

Ron pulled out a stack of business cards belonging to Serena. "This is what those other guys think about your Bees-ness. I found these lying around. Some inside, some outside." He stepped closer to her. "You see, they don't value a treasure such as yourself. But I, however, got your back."

Serena double-gripped Ron's butt cheeks with the famous smirk of arrogance. "And I got yours. Let's ride."

"I drove, but, well, I'll just come back for it later. Hey... you never asked me my name."

"That's okay. It's kinkier that way."

Back at the hotel ballroom, Dyanne was sitting at the table alone, while Wanda and Denise were on the dance floor. They were holding their drinks, bobbing their heads. Every now and then, they would try to dance with some guys.

Sometimes, the ladies succeeded in getting those men to turn around and dance with them. Especially the big men. Other times, the men continued to dance with their guy friends. They might look over their shoulders for a second, but often rejected the idea of dancing with certain women.

Wanda danced with one man, but when his favorite song came on, he spun around to his guy friends and danced with them again. Wanda bobbed her head, then tried to dance elsewhere.

One man danced by himself. Women surrounded him to watch his sexy moves. Denise tried to step up to dance with him, but after a few seconds, the man danced away from her and into the crowd. Denise played off the embarrassment by throwing her hands up, strutting to the bar.

Dyanne said to herself, "Hell. Naw."

♀

The license plate on Serena's Cadillac read: PMPETTE. Ron and Serena were kissing in the back seat. Ron caressed the ghetto queen's tattooed bosom illustrating a bee hive in the shape of a royal palace. Intensity arose.

"Hold on," Serena said. "Not on the leather. Let me take you to my bachelorette pad." Serena and Ron rode together in her car. This pink Cadillac didn't have a great paint job, but had twenty-six inch chromed rims that continuously spun while the car was stopped. Actually, three wheels spun, but one was a bit slow or didn't spin at all.

Ron checked his cellphone, then took out his car charger. "Aw, my battery's dead. May I?"

"Sure, hon. Cigarette lighter's right there. I need to make a stop."

Serena made a sharp turn into a nearby gas station, then stopped at the pump. She snatched out a big knot of money from her purse and handed Ron a fifty-dollar bill.

"I need you to get three big boxes of rubbers," she said.

"Wow, you got big plans, don't you?"

"I always plan big. I like things... big."

"Alright now!"

↬

Ron exited the car and went into the store. Since he was occupied, Serena checked through his cellphone. Ron never found it necessary to setup a pass code for his voicemail feature, so as a result, Serena had access to his inbox. She listened to his voice messages.

The first message: "Hi Ron! This is Raquel. I had such a good time with you yesterday when we... well, you know. Can't wait to do it again!"

(MESSAGE DELETED)

Next message: "Hey, it's Nadine. I'm sorry for what I said to you. I didn't mean it. Let's make up with some hot butt naked sex, alright? You know how I do."

(MESSAGE DELETED)

Next message: "Hi, Ron. It's Carla. I heard the bad news from the guys in the mailroom. Sorry about that. But, we can still hook up, right?"

(MESSAGE DELETED)

Next message: "Mr. Long! It's Luann! I can't wait for you to come back! The office is not the same without you! I have a cake for you, too! It is a red velvet cake that I got from-"

(MESSAGE DELETED)

Next message: "Mr. Long! It's your boss! Pick up! I know you're there! The offer is still up! You're missing out on a lot of money! You know you need it! Come on over here and give me some lovin'! Hell, you screwed everyone else!"

(MESSAGE DELETED)

Next message: "Hey, man. It's me, James. When we were all in the room, doing the mail thing, and getting into all the things we did... you know, the sexual things... I shouldn't have left you hanging like that. No matter what, I always got love for my man. And I'll never forget when you hooked me up. Hit me back up."

(REPLAY MESSAGE)

When Serena replayed James' message, she got excited. She confused the word "mail" with "male".

Serena thought, "The male thing? Bingo!"

↷

Ron returned to the car after purchasing the box of condoms. "Here's your change." He handed Serena her change.

"You're honest. I like that."

"Well, I like that you like that." He checked his phone. "Damn, no messages."

♂

Dyanne, Wanda, and Denise were lounging and having drinks in a booth with three gentleman whom they were just meeting for the first time. Their names were Troy, Leon, and Greg. They seemed like totally masculine men.

"You guys are good dancers!" Wanda said. "Do you come here often?"

Troy answered, "I've been here once before, but this is their first time."

Leon confirmed. "Yeah, I don't usually go to places like this. Troy talked me into it."

"Really?" Wanda asked. "What made you decide to come?"

"They told me that Donna Mayes, the singer, was supposed to be here! I love Donna Mayes! She is so sexy to me! I got all of her albums!"

Dyanne questioned Leon. "Leon, right?"

"Yes."

"I have two questions for you: One, what do you mean when you say, 'places like this'? I'm just curious.

"My other question is, when you see this... Donna Mayes, then what?"

"Well, places like this; Where some women can be so disrespectful! I'm not talking about any of you ladies, but some of these women here are rude." The men nodded their heads in agreement. "Two, if Donna Mayes comes out, I'm gonna see if I can touch her belly!"

Greg gave Leon a fist pound and said, "Lord, yes! She is so fine! If I see her, I would... Oooo!"

"She alright," Denise said. "All she does is beg in her songs. That's why you all like her so much. She's always begging."

"Naw, don't hate! She is fine! I'm going to get her to sign on my chest!" Greg gently pulled apart his shirt near the collar,

‹↗

exposing his upper chest. Denise tried to take a peek at Greg's entire chest. Dyanne looked at Wanda in a way that showed her disapproval. Wanda found nothing wrong with the guys.

"She is sexy, alright," Troy said. "Sexy and paid! But anyway, Dyanne, why weren't you dancing?"

Dyanne answered, "It was too awkward for me. Guys dancing with each other. Wasn't feeling it." The men laughed.

Leon asked Troy, "Did you see that one girl? She was up to no good. Saying some sexual shit in my ear. Looking like a drag king's sister. I almost told her to go somewhere and play with herself."

Dyanne murmured, "Wow..."

"I know, right? You wouldn't believe the things I've heard from chicks! Trust me!"

Greg noticed Dyanne's resentment, unlike Leon. "Why are you so serious?" he asked Dyanne.

"She's not always this serious," Wanda interjected.

Troy said, "Come on, Dyanne, let's dance!" Dyanne accepted.

Troy and Dyanne got up and danced on the dance floor. Troy moved seductively, which was standard, but Dyanne didn't realize the commonality yet. She looked a little confused at first.

Ron laid between the sheets with Serena in her bedroom. The room was filled with the smell of burnt wood from an old, dried up lit stick of incense that once smelled like cherries. She had a faux leopard comforter with silky rayon sheets. It was too warm for a comforter, but she wanted to show it off anyway.

Hovering over her bed was a wide mirror that stretched at about the size of the mattress. Playing in the background was horrible music created by one of the artists of Serena's record label.

"That was good," Serena said. "I'm proud of you, baby."

Ron said, "Um, I'm proud of you, too.

With your... roughness. Never had a woman growl during sex."

"I got a lot of friends, you know. They're all hardcore like me."

"Is that so?"

"I can introduce you to them. They're pretty."

"That's cool, but I'm in no hurry to meet new people."

"But, I'm having a special get-together tomorrow! They'll all be here! Are you busy tomorrow?"

"Actually, I... I took the next two days off."

"What is your name?"

"So, now you ask me." He laughed. "My name is Long. Ron Long."

"Long, baby, I'll let you play with my friends if you stay with me."

"Hmm, let me think... My car's on the other side of town... Pretty friends... Party... Play with friends... Yeah, I'll stay." The two embraced.

♂

Dyanne and Troy returned from the dance floor. They sat where they were previously, in the booth with their friends.

"Are you better now, Dyanne?" Leon asked. "I was wondering if you could handle all that on the dance floor."

"She did good!" Troy said. "Nice rhythm-"

"Wait..." Dyanne said, "Leon, you just said 'handle all that'? Are you talking about your boy here? You see him as all that?"

"Don't twist my words up," Leon said. "You know what I'm saying."

Dyanne laughed along with Leon. She wiped her mouth with her napkin, put the napkin on her lap, then wrote on it with a pen from her purse. She handed the napkin's message to Wanda. Wanda looked at the napkin which read: "Down Low!!" As this went on, the conversation continued.

Leon said, "Troy got those big ole shoulders! I tried to get my shoulders like that, but I can't do it to save my life! I wish I had it like that. All I got is this strong back."

"Shoot, that's all that a sista needs!" Wanda shouted. "Baby got back!"

"But to handle a strong back, you need to know how to work that 'south bend'."

"South who?" Dyanne asked.

"Oh, I know all about the south bend, baby!" Wanda claimed.

Leon replied, "You might **think** you know about it, but there's a lot more to it."

Dyanne asked Wanda, "What the hell is he talking about?"

Being so caught up in the debate, Wanda ignored Dyanne's inquiry and maintained her yap with Leon. "Trust me! I know! You can ask my exes! I put it on them plenty of times!" She counted her pinky finger. "Like with my first husband. He used to be a tomgirl until I hit that south bend on him! He became a man after that, so I know!"

Dyanne asked, "Why is it a damn secret?"

Wanda continued, "Plus, my grip is the tightest! I can damn near open a soda bottle with this thing! Pop!" Wanda raised her arm as if she opened a bottle from her groin.

"Yeah, yeah," Leon said. "That's what they all say. You don't want none of this, because next thing you know, you'll be sucking your thumb in the fetal position." Leon reached into his man bag and pulled out his measuring compass. "You see this?" The compass had a small rubber ball covering the sharp pointed tip. "A woman is going to have to stay within this diameter to satisfy me. Two inches or tighter! Size does matter. Can you handle that?"

Greg instigated. "Uh oh! There goes the compass! Leon does not play!"

Dyanne said, "For someone who's not happy with their own physique, Leon, you sure have high demands."

Greg saw the need to encourage Leon, in spite of Dyanne. "Brother, please. You look good."

"Thank you, brother!" said Leon. Greg's compliment meant more to him than Wanda's.

Then, Greg received a humorous,

sexually explicit picture/text message from a "friend" on his cellphone. It made him laugh, so he showed it to Leon. He also found it funny. They kept it in secret. Denise was curious. Dyanne was annoyed.

"What are you guys getting into after this?" Wanda asked.

"Oh, you wouldn't want to go," said Leon.

"Where?"

Greg answered, "Leon's brother is throwing a toy party. Wanna go? Ha!"

Dyanne asked, "Men have toy parties? For what?"

Leon said, "Fun!" Dyanne was still clueless, so he elaborated. "Look, when I want a fix, I'm not going to depend on a woman to do it for me. Too much come with all of that, so a man has to pump it up sometimes. There's nothing wrong with that."

"I know that's right!" said Greg in his manly tone.

Dyanne asked Leon, "Are you referring to a penis pump? Really?"

Greg intervened. "I got a drawer full of those! A black one, a white one-"

"Actually, I was talking about my doll," Leon said. "She vibrates."

Wanda implied, "Well, I bet it can't do what I can do!"

"I'm not saying it's as good as the real thing, but at least I know I won't catch anything from good ol' Dolly. You never know with some women."

Dyanne sassed Leon. "So a minute ago, it was funny to tell a certain 'chick' to go play with herself, but later on, you have a toy party to go to..."

"Women have their toys, too!" Greg said.

"Hell naw!" Denise shouted. "I'd rather use my fingers than play with a damn toy!"

Dyanne was getting fed up with the discussion. "I'll be back, I'm going to the ladies' room." She got up from her seat and took two and a half steps before realizing that Wanda and Denise stayed seated. She turned around and said, "Come on!" to her friends imperatively. They looked at each

↝

other curiously before following her.

The three women were washing their hands in the ladies room. Club fliers highlighting popular male models from magazine photos were scattered across the countertop. Dyanne looked frustrated!

Wanda was giving advice. "Denise, this guy you speak of, he sounds like a gold-digger to me. Don't spend another penny on his ass! Leave him alone! He doesn't love you, girl!" She faced Dyanne. "But, Dy! I think you got a chance at Troy! He was all on you!"

"Yep," Denise said. "He likes you. I can tell."

"You got the house to yourself, you're off from work, and you're single! And judging by the way he was looking at you, I bet you could get that no later than Friday!"

Denise shouted, "Break that stick!"

Dyanne was totally amazed. "You two... are actually serious." She pondered. "Okay, either I'm crazy or the rest of you are crazy."

Wanda tried to console Dyanne. "Dy, I

know it's hard, but-"

"No! This has nothing to do with Ron!"

"Then, what is the problem?"

"Everything... is backwards! Everyone is acting strange!" Dyanne pointed at Wanda. "You are acting strange." Then, she pointed at Denise. "You're acting strange, and those guys out there are acting **very** strange! Everybody is ass-backwards! And I know I'm not dreaming, because every hour and every minute is accounted for!" She rinsed her hands and flicked water on her face. "Even the people I ran into earlier, they were not behaving normally. I just want things back to the way they were!"

Wanda asked skeptically, "And this has nothing to do with your separation?"

"No. It. Doesn't." Dyanne took a closer look at the fliers on the countertop. "More male models..."

Dyanne, Wanda, and Denise returned from the restroom. There was a loud commotion. They looked to where they were sitting and no one was there. Then, they

↝

followed where the noise was coming from and saw a bunch of men crowded around someone.

"That must be the pop star over there," Denise said. "They might throw their draws in a minute." (For those who don't know, draws are drawers...underwear...duh!)

Security and bodyguards were pushing the men back, demanding them to give the celebrity some room. These men were yelling her name and acting quite fanatically. The women shook their heads, because the guys left them to get a celebrity's autograph.

Dyanne pointed out the disaster. "Do you see that? Do you see that? That is strange!" She rubbed her forehead. "Look, I need some rest. It was fun hanging with you girls. And tell the guys I said thanks for the drinks."

Wanda said, "I bought the drinks."

When Dyanne left her friends behind to make her exit, she passed by another ballroom of the hotel. The doors were wide open. In this ballroom was a late wedding reception/party. Dyanne stopped and watched from the outside.

The groomsmen and other male guests gathered for the garter toss. These men went crazy when they saw the garter in the air! They scrambled for that garter like a fumbled football on the field!

The most aggressive man caught the garter and celebrated. He flexed his biceps and beat his chest like a gorilla. Dyanne's jaw dropped. This man spun the garter in the air like a propeller, then spiked it to the floor like he just ran a touchdown. He chest bumped one of his friends and the guys gave him high fives. Dyanne hurried out of that hotel!

Later that night, Dyanne was dressed for bed. She lifted her pillow and picked up Ron's wedding ring.

She examined the golden ring. "What is happening?" That night, she went to sleep hoping she would wake up out of this long nightmare.

~

Chapter 11ᵗʰ   ॐ

The sunrise illuminated Serena's psychedelic bedroom the next morning. Ron was asleep next to Serena in her bed. She shook Ron out of his sleep. Ron was dreary and could barely open his eyes.

"How about getting up and fixing us some breakfast?" Serena asked.

Ron said drowsily, "Got some milk?"

"Yeah."

"Got cereal?"

"Nope."

"Well, that's all I know how to make. Can't do that other stuff, but I can make a mean bowl of Corn Flakes." He stretched out. "I need to check on my car. Should've drove it here." (Improper... I know.)

"You can't leave, yet! What about the party? You told me last night that you would stick around!"

"I'm kind of burnt out. I've been having way too much fun. But, I'll come back. I promise."

Serena looked very disappointed, then had an idea. "Let me fix you some coffee. You like coffee?"

"In fact I do. I could use a pick-me-up."

In the kitchen, Serena poured Ron some hot coffee into a mug. Then, she peeked over her shoulder while sprinkling a powdery substance into his beverage.

Serena went back to her bedroom, stirring the coffee. She handed the mug to Ron and kissed him on the cheek. Ron took a sip of the drink and gave a nod of satisfaction with a smile. Serena smiled back.

"So tell me, college boy," Serena said, "when you were at the university, have you ever had a male experience?"

"What do you mean?" Ron asked. "Yeah, I

opened mail from the post office if that's what you're talking about."

"Have you ever been with a man?"

"Naw! Why would you ask me that?"

"A lot of men have that bi-curious thing going on in college. Not even a kiss?"

"Not me! Damn, I'm getting dizzy. Can you drop me off?"

"To your car? You can't drive like this. Stay here a little while longer 'til you get better." Ron's vision blurred, then he passed out.

♂

Dyanne sat in her sofa, holding a bagel and a hot beverage. She reached for the remote and turned on the television. On the TV channel was a sitcom where a husband and his wife were arguing.

The husband made a finishing statement. "...Either we spend the funds on our anniversary, or there will be no sex for two weeks..." The studio audience laughed as the wife immediately straightened up her act. Dyanne changed the channel quickly.

↰

On another station, instead of The Ellen Show, there was a show called The Allan Show. He did everything that Ellen does. His studio audience consisted of mostly heterosexual men. There were a handful of lesbian women as well.

"Oh no!" Dyanne said. "They done took Ellen!"

Then, a thought crossed Dyanne's mind. When she first met Darvin Martel, he initiated the handshake between them. That was a showcasing of masculinity, in her view.

Soon afterward, Dyanne drove off into the city streets. In route, she saw the same advertisements with male models, as she did on the previous day. She parked in the shopping mall parking lot.

Still in her house shoes, Dyanne eagerly rushed across the lot to the mall entrance, scaring off seagulls in the process. The birds screamed like those phony, over-acting hussies in porn flicks. Very annoying. There are more seagulls in

↗

parking lots than there are at sea.

Dyanne went to the bookstore where she previously ran into Darvin. She noticed that most of the romance novels were targeting male readers and written by men.

Then, Dyanne surveyed the magazine section, taking note of the many magazines which also targeted men. All instead of the nude magazines. When Dyanne picked up Oprah's magazine, she saw Oprah's boyfriend, Stedman, on the cover. Dyanne fainted.

♀

Around that time, Ron woke up in Serena's bed, again. This time, Serena was not next to him. When he looked ahead to the door, he saw a big man standing there looking at a video on a camera.

"Rise and shine, superstar," the big man said. "You've been busy."

Ron rubbed his eyes. "Who are you? Where is Serena? Why are you standing there?" The big man was focusing on the video. "What are you watching, man? And why am I in my underwear?"

"I'm Armstrong. Serena's not here. I'm holding you here til she gets back. I'm watching a video of the last few hours and you were the life of the party. Take a look..."

Ron got up and watched the camera screen. "Oh my... I didn't know I could... When did she...? Now, that is just nasty!" He covered his mouth. "Aw! I don't remember any of this! Did she just shit?" He paced back and forth. "Armstrong, huh? Where do you know Serena from?"

Armstrong answered, "I met Queen Bees-ness while working at the Player's Pen."

"Oh, you work at the strip club. I've been there quite a few times. So, you're a bouncer?"

"Nope. I'm a stripper. No more questions. Just relax until Her Royal Bees-ness gets back."

Ron scratched his head. "You're a big man. But see, I can't let you keep that video. And I'm not going to stick around here." He looked around. "So, it looks like I

⤳

might have to kick your ass. How about you put that camera down and get ready..."

"Hm... How about I just hold this camera while whooping your ass and have it all on tape?"

"Well, you see, that would put me at an advantage. You'll never know-"

Ron hit him with a sucker punch. This forced Armstrong's head back, but only for him to swing forward with a countering head butt, knocking Ron out cold.

What seemed like moments later, Ron woke up for the third time that day! He saw the blurry sight of Luann trying her best to revive him. She waved in his face while calling his name. She even gave him sloppy mouth-to-mouth resuscitation.

"Mr. Long!" Luann chanted, as she would normally do at the office. "Wake up, sleepy head!"

Ron squinted. "L-Luann? What in the world are you doing here? Ow! My head hurts!"

"I'm here for love! Ready to get my swerve

on! Hee, hee!"

"Get your swerve on? Uh, there must have been a mistake. How did you find out I was here?"

"I got a call from your phone. It was a friend of yours. She was speaking in that Ebonics language. I haven't studied that one much." She saw how upset Ron was. "It was cool, because she likes to rhyme and when she said business, it sounded more like bee's nest. Like a BZZZ, you know?"

"She shouldn't have asked you to come here. But since you did, I need to borrow money for cab fare."

"So we're not going to...?"

"No, Lu."

"Wait a minute! You're supposed to perform for me! I spent a lot of money for this!"

"You spent money? What! Aw, hell naw! This broad is pimping me! She's pimping me?" He pounded himself on the head out of frustration. "Tell me, who's out there?"

"Just the big guy who let me in. He keeps

watching something on his video camera."

"That bastard caught me slippin'. I got to find a way out of here. That's what I get for messing around!" Luann started to cry. "Come on, Luann. You're better than this."

"Apparently, I'm not!" she yelled. "You ignore me all the time! No matter how nice I am to you! I do nothing wrong! I try to be the best person I can be and that's not good enough!" She stomped her foot out of anger. "You'd rather give attention to women who don't even like you! Just because they're prettier than me! Am I that disgusting to you?"

"No, Luann. That's not the-"

"Liar! I'm not stupid, Ron! I'm not what you want. Just say it! But, it's not just you. It's the rest of these men, too! Just because I don't have a flashy car and I catch the bus!" She removed her glasses to wipe her tears.

"Yeah I live with my mom," she said, "but who else will take care of her except for me? Out of four children, I'm the only one who cares and she calls me the disappointment! It's because of people like you!"

"But, Luann-"

"I try and try, and try. Who's going to love me?" She whimpered. "Nobody wants to hold me! I hate my life! I wish I had the guts to end it all!"

"Please don't talk that way, Luann."

Armstrong yelled from behind the closed door, "Is everything okay in there? Do I have to come in there?"

"Keep your ass outside!" Luann shouted. Armstrong carefully backed away from the door.

Ron removed the shade off of a lamp that was positioned on the nightstand. "Lu, if you help me out of here, I will do something very special for you." He unplugged the lamp.

Luann wiped her tears and smiled widely again. "What do you want me to do, Mr. Long?" She put her glasses back on.

Ron walked to the side of the door which would mask him behind it when opened.

↷

"Call that big bastard in."

Luann screamed as loud as she could, then gave Ron a thumbs up. Ron looked at her like she was crazy.

Armstrong charged in. "What's been going on in here? Where is-"

Bang! Ron hit Armstrong in the head with the lamp, knocking him unconscious. Ron hurried to put on his clothes, then left the bedroom with Luann.

The video camera was sitting on the coffee table. Ron took it right away. When he did, the front door opened. Enter Serena.

She saw Ron and Luann making their exit with the video camera in hand. "Where are you two going with my camera?" She faced Luann, pointing at Ron. "You handled that, already?"

"You pimped me, you fake ass Hue Heffa!" Ron shouted. "You actually pimped me!"

"And you liked it, hoe! Now go back in there and wait for some more chicks. Did you meet my... hold up."

Serena looked in the bedroom and witnessed Armstrong laying on the floor knocked out next to the shattered lamp. She reached in her purse and flicked out a switchblade.

Ron ordered, "Serena, put that away and give me my wallet. I don't believe in hitting women, but I will defend myself."

Serena stepped closer to Ron with the blade. "First, I'm gonna cut ya. Then, I'm gonna pimp slap the taste out yo mouth! Now, go back in there and make my monaaay!" (translated: money)

Luann circled around, putting Serena in between them. Serena shifted back and forth, monitoring both Ron and Luann's movements. Then suddenly, Luann did martial arts warm-ups like they do in karate movies. She executed the moves like a pro, then went into her fighting stance.

Serena observed Luann's knowledge of the arts and dropped her blade. "Hell naw, she know her shit. I ain't messin' with her. Here, you take your wallet. I'll give you a ride out of here!"

Ron and Luann looked at each other perplexedly. Serena took the car keys out of her purse and headed straight to the door.

"Come on," Serena said. "Y'all gotta go."

Luann was cheerful. "I call shotgun!" Ron followed Serena and Luann out of the apartment.

♂

Dyanne arrived to the area of the beach where she first met Darvin. He was there with the book club that he is a part of. He read one of his poems out loudly to his peers. Darvin hoped to someday fulfill his dream of reading his poetry in front of large audiences, such as The Penis Monologues. He was reading in character, totally different from his usual demeanor. Dyanne only heard the ending.

Darvin's closing words were, "...baby. But how do I make love, when love makes me go crazy?"

The audience applauded. Dyanne was bewildered by the last words of Darvin's poem. She didn't get it, but when she and Darvin made eye contact, she clapped along with everyone else.

Darvin walked over to Dyanne and greeted her. They separated from the crowd.

"Darvin, these last two days have been difficult for me," Dyanne said. "I woke up to a different world. Nothing has been in my favor and I feel abandoned by everyone who was my friend before then. It's like I don't even know them anymore.

"I really can't explain this, and this might not make sense to you, but you have been a positive light. I know I was hard on you yesterday, but I really do appreciate you.

"You are the only person who made me feel normal. I don't know how to cope without someone like you right now."

Darvin replied, "You did nothing wrong yesterday. You stood up to me, that's all. You were true to yourself. That's what I like, a strong woman with a little street in her." He put his left hand on Dyanne's right shoulder. "Dyanne, you are a sweet person.

A good girl. I like you as a friend, but not like that."

"Like what?" Dyanne asked him while carefully removing his hand from her shoulder.

"You know. We just met yesterday and you're showing a lot of your feelings. I'm not ready for all of that. Plus, I usually go for the adventurous type. The 'hood chicks. I have a weakness for bad girls."

Dyanne was shocked and offended, at first. But as she thought more about it, she found Darvin's words insanely hilarious!

Dyanne tried to talk, in spite of how hard she was laughing. "Let me get this straight... HAAHAAA!" She hunched over, holding her gut laughing. "Excuse me, but this is a bit much. So let me guess, you feel more protected when you're with a 'hood chick', don't you?"

"Yes, I do. One who is not afraid to defend with you and has street smarts. I don't want to get caught in an altercation, then look for her, and she takes off running."

Dyanne laughed until she coughed. Tears of laughter were rolling down her face.

She cleared her throat. "Boy was I wrong about you!"

"Why is it so funny?" Darvin asked.

"Okay, for one thing, look at you! There is nothing 'hood about you! You read romance novels! You're a nice guy! And you want a 'hood-chick'?

"These women you fell for in the past; were they gang members? Drug dealers? Did they ever beat you?" She could not stop laughing. "And then you say 'protected'? Protected from what? Walking dark alleys? Are you in trouble? Why are strangers always trying to kick your ass?"

Dyanne paused for second after catching her breath. "Oh! I know what it is! You need a woman to squash bugs for you! Hahaa!"

Darvin was highly upset. "You know what? I was almost going to give you a chance! Almost! But, you blew it!" He finger-pointed her at eye level. "When you stood up to me, I thought you had potential! I felt you weren't a push-over! But since you want to laugh and insult me like a little girl," he took the index finger he used to point at her and pointed down towards his lower regions, "then you'll never get none of this! You had your chance! Probably couldn't hang anyway..."

Darvin stormed off. Dyanne burst out laughing again. She had her laugh of the day. Maybe of the week.

Serena, Ron, and Luann rode up to Ron's car, which had an Abandoned Vehicle sticker on its window.

"Here we are," said Serena.

Ron opened the car door. "Thank you. Whatever your real name is."

"So, you're going to keep the whole camera? Just take the memory chip!"

Ron removed the memory chip and gave the camera to Serena. The look on his face showed that he totally despised her.

Luann exited the car, saying, "Thanks for

the ride, Bee's nest! BZZ, B-BZZZ, BZZZ!"

Serena said to Ron, "Man, I'm scared of her. That bitch is crazy! You be careful, 'cause you're easy to fool."

She flipped out a fold of cash. "Here's your cut, baby." Ron exited the car without taking the money.

He said through her driver's side window, "Condoms or no condoms, I'm getting checked. You better hope that it comes out negative, and you better be glad my ass ain't hurtin'."

Serena yelled out of her window after Ron stepped away. "Keep it harder, hoe!" She drove off aggressively.

↝↗

Chapter 12th ⚚

*I*t was getting dark when Ron drove Luann to her home. They had already grabbed something to eat after leaving the nightclub parking lot, where Ron's car was left overnight.

Luann greeted her mother. "Mom, I'm home!" Luann's mom grunted. "Guess what, mom! I brought company! That's why I'm here so late. This is Ron!"

"Pleased to meet you," Ron said to the elderly lady in his deep baritone voice.

Luann's mom turned away from the television and saw Ron. She sat there in disbelief! Ron extended his hand for her, but she couldn't move. She was stunned!

↜

Luann said, "We'll be in my room, Ma. See ya later! Hee, hee."

Ron and Luann were sitting at the foot of her bed. "So, where did you learn moves like that?" Ron asked. "The kicking and the spinning."

"The internet," Luann said. "That was the only thing I learned so far. Can't actually fight. I just learned that to try to pick up guys. It's working!"

"Well aren't you a player." There was a long, silent pause. They were just looking around.

"Want to play this new online game I started?" Luann asked.

"Um, sure. What type of game is it?"

"It's called Sperminator 3: Rise of the Sex Machines! It's Rated M for mature!"

"Okay. I'll play this with you. An online porn action video game. Interesting."

Luann became excited and jittery. She activated the surround sound speaker volume before playing the game. This game had corny dialogue. The Game Audio voice sounded like a bad impersonation of Arnold Schwarzenegger.

Game Audio: "Cum with me if you want to live."

Luann said, "See, that's cum with a U in place of the O. Get it?"

Ron said unenthusiastically, "Yes, Luann. I get it."

Luann was really into the game. She trash talked and hollered throughout. She even jumped on the bed like a kid. The game had a series of moaning and groaning, along with other sexual sound effects.

Luann's mom rolled up in her wheelchair to Luann's bedroom door and listened in through a shot glass. When she heard the sound effects and Luann's outbursts, she thought they were having wild sex in the bedroom. A big, pleasant smile shined upon her face. She jumped in her seat with every sudden loud noise coming from the room.

"Take that, bitch!" Luann screamed.

Game Audio: "I'm cumming... I lied." There was a loud female moan. "Hot-stellar-vista, baby." An explosion blasted through the voluminous speakers causing Luann's mom to drop the shot glass.

Luann yelled, "Shoot! Got me right in the face!" Luann's mom was amazed at what she heard! "Thanks, Mr. Long! That was fun!"

"No, Luann," Ron replied. "Thank you for helping me with Serena. And for the many times you were kind to me. But most of all, thank you for being the same Luann for all of these days. Don't ever change."

"Aww, that is so sweet!"

"Have you ever been kissed?"

"By my dog. That was before he ran away."

"I really think you should wait for someone perfect for you. Not wait in the house, but go somewhere you can be seen. I'm sure you'll find someone who wants you for you. I would just take advantage of you."

"That's cool."

"No, Luann. It's not. Believe me, you don't want to be taken advantage of. But, I'll give you something special just as I promised. Something to build your confidence. Close your eyes..."

Luann closed her eyes and puckered her lips, expecting a kiss. Ron looked at her face and squirmed. Instead of kissing her on the lips, he kissed her neck. Luann gazed to the ceiling as her jaw was hanging like a lopsided chandelier. Her eyes rolled.

Then suddenly, she started to climax. She kicked out her legs, causing a slipper to fly off of her right foot. After her joyful moment, she laid back on the bed, remaining where she sat.

Ron was shocked! "Did you just...? Tell me you didn't just... Well, I guess you don't have to wait for that now, do you?"

Luann snored. Ron looked and found her fast asleep! He could not believe it! So, he put her on the pillow and laid there with her in his arms. This was so she wouldn't feel left alone.

Luann's mom was asleep in her wheelchair just outside of Luann's bedroom door. Ron's cellphone vibrated on the dresser.

The caller ID read "Wife". But by this time, Ron was also asleep.

Dyanne got the default voicemail greeting from Ron's phone. It prompted her to leave a message.

"Ron, it's me," Dyanne said. "We need to talk. I promise not to yell at you, or cut you off, or any of that. I just hope that you're willing to do the same." The cellphone beeped.

The alarm clock went off at 6:00am. Ron was still with Luann. Luann hit the alarm button, then rolled over to face Ron. He was awake as well.

"Mr. Long?" Luann asked. "Did we, uh... Did we...?"

Ron patronized her. "Yes, Lu. And it was great." Luann rolled on her back and gave out a sigh of relief along with a huge grin. "Getting ready for work, Luann?"

"No, I took the day off. Just forgot about the alarm clock."

↝

Ron curiously hesitated. "Well. You should use this opportunity to go out. Enjoy the Spring. I'll give you a ride to the park."

"I would love that! Wow! You're so kind! I'll get ready."

Ron grabbed his items off of Luann's dresser then proceeded to the bedroom door. When he opened the door, he saw Luann's mom sleeping in her wheelchair just outside of the room.

"Um, Luann!" Ron called out. "I do have room for a third person!"

Later, Luann stepped outside of the house, followed by Ron pushing Luann's mom in her wheelchair. When they got to the car, Luann's mom looked back to take a look at her house. She was surprised by the color!

Luann's mom shouted, "Purple! Purple!"

"Yes, mom!" Luann cheered. "See? It was purple all along!"

Then, her mom said in a low tone, "...No man wants a damn purple house."

They made it to the park. Luann and her

mom were outside of Ron's car, ready to explore.

"Thank you so much for this!" Luann said to Ron. "I'll never forget it!" She almost left, but turned back around. "Oh! About last night…" She ducked her head through Ron's car window. "I know you're still feeling the aftereffects of our passion, but I still need to take care of my mom. She comes first, you know?" Ron said nothing. "Now, don't get too sobby about it. You'll get through this. I know I put my mack down, but we got to keep this…" She whispered. "On the low-low. Okay? Hot-stellar-vista… baby! Hee, hee!"

Ron laughed to himself when Luann walked away. Luann turned around to wave, but she stumbled. She didn't quite fall. She waved successfully after regaining control of herself. Ron waved back.

Ron checked his cellphone and saw that Dyanne called him the night before. He drove off immediately after listening to the message.

↝

13ᵗʰ Chapter

Dyanne waited on her living room sofa before the doorbell rang. She opened the door to let Ron in. They sat across from each other. Dyanne placed Ron's wedding ring on the table between them. Ron did the same with Dyanne's ring.

"Well," Dyanne said. "Anything special happen since you kept my ring?"

Ron replied, "I wouldn't say special, but... as a matter of fact, yes. I learned quite a few things. What about you?"

"I've gained more perspective."

"Have you talked to the pastor?"

"No. More importantly, I think we need to talk. Do you remember what you said when you gave me this ring?"

"Honestly, I don't. I just repeated what I was told to say."

"Same here. So... what did you learn?"

"I learned that for all we've been through, I don't have much worth complaining about. I realize how much of a jackass I've been. And worst of all, that I wasn't being a good example to our son. Oh, and he watches porn on the computer."

"Porn? Is that so?"

"Yeah, we talked about it. I also learned that getting plenty of attention from the opposite sex is over-rated. I thought I was missing something when we were together, but I was dead wrong."

"Plenty of attention? I hardly got any attention. Does that seem odd to you?"

"...Very."

Dyanne pondered. Ron pondered. They both spoke at the same time. "We need our rings back!" They laughed together, then regained composure.

Then, Dyanne said, "I don't know about the marriage thing, though. I don't see it."

↬

Ron addressed her concern. "Dyanne. All we ever wanted was to make things right for our children. I've done a bad thing. I understand that now. But, we are still parents.

"Marriage doesn't make or break that part. But if I had to do it all over again, I would have married you. Except for this time, I would remember every thing I said when giving you this ring."

"Me too. So, where does this leave us?"

"Nowhere, yet. Let's just see where life takes us. Maybe what we learned will bring us closer, or maybe it'll pull us further apart. Who knows? But, let's not rush it this time. You can't force Love when Love is a force of its own."

Dyanne smiled. "You're right. I like that. Yeah, I see you've changed. But like you said, we shouldn't rush anything. That includes the divorce proceedings." She handed Ron his ring back. "Let's take what we learned and use that when raising our children. That's what it was all about in the first place, right?"

"Yes it was." He handed Dyanne her ring. "You know... I can't wait to have that talk with Marla."

"And I can't wait to talk to Ronnie!" They laughed and carried on with their stories.

Outside in the city streets, a billboard advertisement changed from a male model back to a female model.

The End ♣